# THE TRICK —OR— TREAT CORPSE

THE FOUR SEASONS BOOK ONE · FALL

# THE TRICK —OR— TREAT CORPSE

## RANDOLPH CREW

ARTEC

Published by Artec Publishing
Copyright © 2022 by Randolph E. Crew

PCN: 0-9651430-1-52
ISBNs:  978-0-9651430-0-4 (eBook)
        978-0-9651430-1-1 (Paperback)

Edited by Kristen Corrects, Inc.
Cover and interior design by Roseanna White Designs

First edition published 2022

OTHER BOOKS BY RANDOLPH E. CREW

*A Killing Shadow*
*One-Way Mission*

*For Phillip, my well-read son*

# TABLE OF CONTENTS

# PROLOGUE

My name is Nathan B. Hawke. I'm from Dallas, Texas, and for thirty-seven years, I solved murders. While my career as a homicide detective may have officially started in Dallas, it actually began when I was in junior high school in Southern Pines, North Carolina. I had a reputation in those days that inhibited my crime-scene credibility, but… Well, let me explain it this way: From the fall of 1955 through the summer of 1956, I came across four dead bodies. Not one of them had died by any act of God; none had been washed up by a tsunami or zapped by lightning. They were murdered. When the local police wouldn't act on my information (that credibility thing), I tried to solve the murders myself. That's when my murder-solving career began.

I'm retired now, and I want to tell you about all four of those murders in a series of books called the *Four Seasons* series. I'll use my perspective from that time, and I'll start with the body my dog and I found deep in "Boris" Barrow's woods. That was on the Friday before Halloween, 1955, and I call it the case of the *Trick-or-Treat Corpse*.

# CHAPTER 1
## THE CORPSE

Late that Friday afternoon, dressed in jeans and my lucky blue-striped T-shirt, I sat on the concrete stoop of our two-bedroom brick house, drummed my fingers on my knees, and waited for Mom to get home with her decision. Neither of us realized at the time that her decision that day, and my actions based on her decision, would set the course for me for the rest of my life.

Superman, my beady-eyed, bowlegged mutt, sat on his haunches beside me and watched two squirrels chase each other around the longleaf pine in our front yard. That dog, believe it or not, had a cowlick just like mine, but his was a dirty tan located in the dead center of his forehead. Mine was, at that time in my life, sandy blond and on my left side where I parted my short hair. I wasn't happy about being the only one in the family, or the sixth grade, with a cowlick, but when Granddaddy pointed out that Albert Einstein had a cowlick, I felt better about it—not happy, just better. At least I had Mom's brown eyes.

Out of sight behind me, because I didn't want Mom to think I was too sure of what her decision would be, I had strategically placed my late father's old slingshot and his military-issue binoculars.

As I leaned over to retie the frayed laces on my Converse high-tops, I saw our sky-blue Ford finally appear down our quiet street. As it passed through the late afternoon shadows of oaks ready to drop their leaves with the next gust of October wind, I could see Mom at the wheel. Her arm rested on the bottom of the open window frame while a few stray hairs danced around her still-tanned face. I'd served my sentence, but her normally full lips, now squeezed tight, told me the next few minutes might not go my way. I glanced up to the heavens and crossed my fingers.

As she turned into the driveway, I stood and brushed Superman's hair from my shirt and jeans. The Ford, the car my dad had bought for us before he left for Korea a few years before, crunched to a stop on the hard-packed gravel.

Superman and I jogged over to her where I thought I'd ease into the conversation by showing an interest in her.

"How was work, Mom?" I smiled. "Can I go now?"

She switched off the engine and dropped the car keys into her black purse. She looked at me.

"Nate, are we clear on why you were confined to quarters this week?"

Mom liked to use Dad's old Marine Corps expressions to make a point; unfortunately, I'd heard that one a lot.

"Yes, ma'am. Very clear. No more stories."

"*Lies*, Nate. No more lies."

"Yes, ma'am, no more lies. Just the truth, the whole truth, and nothing but the truth."

Her dimples deepened as she fought back a smile.

"Thank you, Judge Nathan."

She sat up straighter as if to regain the stern mother look.

"Nate, listen to me… Honesty is the best policy. It is *always* the best policy. I will never punish you for telling me the truth. Do you read me this time? Do you understand me?"

Superman's pointed tail banged against my leg as if to say, *Listen up, Boss.*

I glanced at Superman and then back to Mom.

"Yes, ma'am, loud and clear. I understand."

"So, there's no need to lie to me or exaggerate to me or deceive me, Nate. I'm on your side! But I can't keep claiming your innocence only to be shot down by your principal when he produces eyewitness statements contradicting your side of the story!"

"I know, Mom, but that won't happen again. Honest."

"So, there won't be any more imaginary bullies stealing your homework? No more mysterious thieves stealing raw eggs from the school kitchen then slipping one into Rose's purse?"

"No, ma'am, never again, but Mom… Tom Ray really does

steal kids' homework, and that egg would have been harmless if Rose hadn't hit me with her basket purse. That's what broke the egg!"

She pursed her lips and shook her head.

"Nate?"

"Yes, ma'am, I know; she wouldn't have hit me if I hadn't banged on the back of her chair and made her mad."

"Thank you."

She opened the car door, stepped out, swung it closed behind her, then straightened her green cotton dress. She raised and smiled.

"You have a great imagination, Nate…."

She reached over and groomed my cowlick, a motherly habit I'd grown to accept.

"And you're very creative. But in the future, please apply those gifts usefully, not maliciously. Copy that?"

She held out her arms.

I tucked my head into her chest in a hug.

"Solid copy, Mom, and I'm sorry. Really, it won't happen again."

"Well, it better not. Where are you going, Barrow's woods?"

"Yes, ma'am."

"Why? What are you up to?"

"I'm on a secret mission."

I pointed to Dad's binoculars on the stoop and whispered, "Reconnaissance."

"Recon, huh? Okay, you can go, but be home before dark."

"And I can go to Mary Elizabeth's Halloween party Monday night?"

She smiled.

"Of course. I wouldn't want to disappoint Mary Elizabeth."

"Thank you, Mom, thank you!"

I hugged her again and then looked down at Superman.

"Come on, you super dog, let's hit the woods."

I retrieved the binoculars and slingshot, looped the strap of the binoculars over my head, and led Superman across our yard and toward the woods on the other side of the street.

Edged by tall grass and blackberry bushes, the woods were mostly tall red oaks plus a few longleaf pines, a sprinkling of dogwoods—now already showing their red fall colors—and a huge magnolia tree you could see from the road. We called it "The Lookout" because it was easy to climb, and from the top, we could see most of the houses on our block. The woods were about five acres, or so I'd been told.

All five acres belonged to old man Barrow. My friends called him "Boris" Barrow because he looked like Boris Karloff, the actor in horror movies like *Frankenstein* and *The Body Snatcher,* movies I wasn't allowed to see. "They'll give you nightmares," my mother said. I snuck in to see them anyhow, and she was right; I did have a few restless nights after *The Body Snatcher.*

I'd never met Mr. Barrow, never even seen him, and I

doubted Horrible Charlie, Mary Elizabeth, the Fryfogels, or any of my other friends had either. He lived back in his woods down a long, curved driveway in an old Victorian stone house with tall turrets on either end of a long, dark porch. It even had a widow's walk above the second floor.

Vinnie Marcello was probably the most reliable source of information on Mr. Barrow because Vinnie lived in the big house next to the Barrow property. But Vinnie was a teenager like my sister and thus not that reliable when it came to telling the truth to kids like me. So, I didn't know; maybe Mr. Barrow didn't look like Boris Karloff.

To our right, and beside the streetlight on the other side of the street from our next-door neighbor's house, a thin trail led into the woods. It was still half overgrown with thorny blackberry bushes, so Superman and I chose to walk past the light and go farther down to old man Barrow's sandy dirt driveway. That is, *I* chose to walk past the light. Superman chose to stop and do some serious sniffing and then leave his mark on the telephone pole that also served as a light post. He joined me three houses down as I turned left and along the left side of Mr. Barrow's drive.

The mission was to get another look at that huge shadow of a flying thing I'd seen above the woods the week before, but this time through heavy lenses. My plan was to take the driveway as far as the old carriage house and then, before we could be seen from the big house, duck behind the carriage house and cut into the woods.

That was the plan, but about halfway down the drive and just as I entered the long shadows from the pine trees on the other side of the drive, and with the carriage house still twenty yards away, Superman slammed on the brakes and held his plum-red nose in the air.

I took a sniff, but all I smelled was the hint of burning leaves from Vinnie's backyard.

Superman lowered his nose to the ground.

*Uh-oh, here we go again.*

I pointed at him.

"Stay, Superman, stay!"

He looked at me like, *Not now, Nathan my boy.*

He took off to our left and through the tall grass, his pit bull rump driving his bloodhound wrinkled body, ears flapping.

I ran after him. Grass whipped my faded jeans, sweat popped out under my T-shirt, and my sister's voice screamed in my head, *You should have brought the leash, you moron!* Yeah, that plus I should have remembered what an undisciplined mutt I was dealing with.

At the tree line, I jumped a rotten log, ran into the woods between a couple of tall pines, then chased after the sound of Superman's baying. The baying sounded more like a moan with a woof-like sound at the end, like he couldn't decide if he was a baying hound or a barking dog.

"Come here, Superman, come!" I yelled between breaths as if he would actually obey me.

Of course, he didn't obey me, but fifty yards into the woods, now darkened by the kind of wicked shadows I'd seen in those horror movies, the bay-bark stopped, and all I could hear was my panting and my tennis shoes pounding the dried leaves and twigs on the forest floor.

Then I popped out into a small clearing, and there he was, sniffing a lump on the ground.

As I jogged closer, I could see the lump was actually…a body, a man's body on its right side with its knees drawn up in a fetal position. Flies buzzed around it.

I slowed to a stop and stared, eyes wide and still adjusting to the darkness.

I took another couple of steps, stopped, scanned the area, and then stepped up to the body.

I kicked its top knee and jumped back.

Nothing…stiff.

But it was definitely a man, a man with wavy blond hair dressed in gray slacks and a white shirt with dark stains around his unbuttoned collar. A blue tie hung loosely around his neck. I bent down and swatted the flies away.

And he had a black hole in his head just above his left ear.

I popped erect, now a little woozy, and pointed at the ground beside me.

"Superman, come here!"

From the other side of the body, he raised his head, ran his tongue over his upper lip, and looked at me like he was giving my command due consideration, but it definitely conflicted with his desire to stay on the scene, so, therefore...

I ripped the leather belt from my jeans, then leaped over the body and grabbed Superman by his leather collar. I held the collar and looked around us.

For some reason, I felt eyes on me.

I looped my belt under his collar and then dragged that fifty-pound, year-old-but-still-puppy-brained dog from the scene and back to the sandy-clay driveway as fast as I could.

A few minutes later, my T-shirt soaked in sweat, my white socks and Superman's legs covered in beggar's lice, I jogged up the two steps to our front door.

I reached for the brass doorknob, but before I could grab it, the tall and always-unhappy Bossy Becky yanked it open. She pointed at me with her Wicked Witch of the West finger.

"You!" she said. "Get in here!"

I stepped in with Superman beside me. He held his head and his pointed tail high like he expected an ovation from Becky for his day's work. She ignored him.

I slid my belt off his collar and looked around the house,

quiet except for Little Richard singing "Tutti Frutti" on the radio in the bedroom Becky shared with Mom.

"Where's Mom? Where's Granddaddy?"

She slammed the door behind me.

"They're at The Pig. And you, Mr. Naughty Nate, were supposed to be home by dark. Remember?"

I marched across the carpeted living room and tossed the binoculars and slingshot in the corner of the sofa on the far wall.

"So, it's not completely dark yet—no big deal. Look, I've got to get to the phone."

In the hallway, I hung a left, walked through the dining room then into the kitchen. Becky walked right behind me, poking me in the shoulder.

I knocked her hand away.

"Lay off me, Becky. This is serious."

At the far wall and the end of the gray vinyl counter near the kitchen table, I opened the drawer with the phone book inside.

"I found a dead man, Becky…that is, Superman found a dead man."

I lifted the receiver off the black phone on the counter and looked down at Superman.

"Isn't that right, Superman?"

He looked up at Becky, rolled in his tongue, and I swear he grinned.

"Bull!"

I fingered the number Mom had written on the cover of the phone book and dialed.

"No bull! I'm tellin' ya; this is serious!"

The phone rang once, then, "Southern Pines Police Department, Lewis."

"Hey, Officer Lewis, great, I'm glad it's you. This is Nathan Hawke, Mrs. Hawke's—"

"Connie's boy, right?"

"Yes, sir, that's right. Look, Officer Lewis, I ah...well, I know you're not going to believe this, but...well...."

I shrugged.

"Well...I just found a dead man in Barrow's woods."

I blew out a breath.

I heard him snicker and then cup the mouthpiece like he was saying something to someone in the office. I heard his hand slide away.

"A dead man, huh, Nate?"

"Yes, sir, a dead man with a hole in his head, like a bullet hole."

He snickered again.

"Like a bullet hole, huh?"

"Yes, sir. Look, Officer Lewis, this is not a prank, and I'm not lying. Please. The man is dead and if you want to know where he is, I can lead you there."

"Nate, is your mother home?"

"No, sir."

"Grandfather?"

"No, sir."

"Well, Nate, listen…let me call the chief on this, and I'll get back to you. I've got your number. Meanwhile, when your mother gets back have her call me, okay?"

"Yes, sir." I hung up.

Becky pulled out a chair and sat at the red Formica and steel kitchen table. She looked down at Superman then up at me, her blue eyes as wide as if she'd seen Elvis standing there. She brushed the bangs out of her eyes and pulled her brown hair back over her ears.

"You, ah…you really did find a body, didn't you?"

For the first time, I noticed her eyes were roughly outlined with some kind of cheap eyeliner like she'd been practicing in the mirror when she saw me coming.

"Yeah, we really did."

I stared at her, mesmerized by how stupid she looked. *Man, why do girls do crap like that?*

"Well? Is he coming?"

"Who, Officer Lewis?"

"Yeah, is good ol' boy Quick Draw Louie headed this way?"

I stepped toward the backdoor.

"No, not yet, and hey, he's a good guy—why do you call him names?"

"'Cause he slapped leather on Vinnie one time, that's why! Like he was John Wayne or something."

I stopped.

"Vinnie probably had it coming, probably flipped out that switchblade on Lewis, the same blade he likes to flash at us kids. Vinnie's dangerous, Becky, can't you see that?"

"No, he's a good-lookin' guy who doesn't take crap off anybody—not teachers and not cops."

She smiled.

"Besides, I think the knife is cool."

She held out her hand and examined her hot pink fingernails.

"And he has other cool things too."

I shook my head and took the last two steps to the backdoor. Talking to her was like beating my head against the trunk of the tallest oak tree in Barrow's woods.

She stood.

"Wait a minute. Where are you going?"

"To put Superman away and get him some water."

"Okay, go ahead and take care of your stupid mutt."

She stood and reached for the phone.

"I'm callin' Vinnie."

I had reached for the leather leash on the hook by the backdoor but quickly spun around.

"No, Becky! Don't call Vinnie! That grease-ball will just

run over there and screw everything up—mess up clues and all that stuff."

"No, he won't."

"Yeah, he will! He'll do it just to show off for you, show what a brave man he is. Please don't call him; just wait for Mom."

I flicked on the outside light and opened the door. Superman brushed past me.

She picked up the receiver and dialed.

"Shut up. I'm callin'."

Outside I heard our car pull into the driveway, and from the kitchen counter I heard, "Hey, Vinnie. Becky."

# CHAPTER 2
## THE MAN IN THE WINDOW

Behind the house, the white double doors to our single-car garage lit up with each bounce of the Ford's headlights. The car ground to a stop, and the lights and engine died. Mom opened her door, which illuminated the light on the cabin ceiling, and Granddaddy pushed on his passenger door.

I waved from the back doorstep.

"Mom, I've got to talk to you."

She closed her door.

"Be right there."

Granddaddy closed his door and walked toward the garage. He used the old garage as his workshop, and I suspected he also used it to get away from us—especially Becky. He was secretive about it, even kept it padlocked. But hey, he was just a secretive kind of guy. I didn't mind because I shared the other bedroom with him, so his private space worked out well for both of us. While he was in the garage, I could do homework, build my model airplanes, or conduct my experiments.

Meanwhile, there was still that body in the woods, and Mom still needed to call Officer Lewis.

Mom opened the trunk with a snap, and the trunk light came on.

Superman stood beside me, but when he heard the trunk lid open, his ears perked up. He turned his head toward Mom like, *What'd ya bring me, huh? Dog biscuits?*

He trotted over to the car, now only vaguely lit by the light by the backdoor.

I retrieved his water bowl from the pen. The pen, which Granddaddy and I had built and nicknamed the Superman Suite, was a U-shape chain link fence around the brick wall on the back of our house. It was laid out beside the faucet and just to the right of the backdoor as you exit. The entrance gate faced the faucet. On the inside, we had built a floor using pallets from the city dump, and then we built a doghouse out of scrap lumber, boards Granddaddy had gotten from a friend at the VFW. It even had a green shingle roof. The result was a nice, cozy, high-and-dry house with a sundeck.

While I filled his water bowl, I turned toward Mom.

"I'll get the bags in a minute."

I turned off the water.

"Got something to tell you, Mom. Something important."

I walked into the pen and put the bowl on the deck.

Standing behind the trunk, Mom tossed a dog biscuit toward Superman, and he caught it in midair. And right there was the problem: Superman the Mooch got treats whether he obeyed commands or not. I'd been meaning to talk to Mom about that. I stepped out through the gate and waited by the backdoor.

Now with her black purse over one arm and holding a bag of groceries against her green dress, she walked up to me with a half-grin.

"How important is it, Nate?"

The grin got bigger; she liked to tease, and Dad had loved that about her.

"Is it life or death?"

I grinned back at her.

"Actually, my dear mother…it's death."

I lost the grin and locked eyes with her.

"Honest, Mom, it really is death—as in murder."

I pointed toward the street.

"Over there in the woods, I found a dead man, I mean a stone-cold dead man, as in stiff!"

I shrugged.

"So, probably murder. Anyhow, I ran home and called Officer Lewis about it, and he wants you to call him as soon as you get in."

I opened the backdoor for her and stepped back onto the step.

"And please, Mom, please call him right away; he's waiting on your call."

She stepped inside, stopped, and looked back at me without the grin.

"A body? A corpse in Mr. Barrow's woods?"

I grimaced and nodded.

"Yes, ma'am."

She shook her head.

"Nate, don't lie to me. You promised, remember?"

"Yes, ma'am, I remember, but this is no lie, Mom. Honest."

She studied my face a second.

"So, you're really serious."

"Yes, ma'am. Deadly serious."

From the kitchen, I heard the receiver hit the base and Becky say, "Hi, Mom. What'd you bring me?"

I smirked. *Dog biscuits, I hope.*

Mom glanced over at Becky.

"Rations and other necessities of life."

She looked back at me.

"Okay, Nate, I'll call. Meanwhile, you go get the rest of the groceries."

She hooked her heel around the door and closed it with a swing of her open-toe black pump.

From the garage, I heard keys jingle and the padlock snap, but I stood on the step and kept my eyes on Mom and Becky. I could see them through the glass panes in the door. Mom glanced at the sink to her right.

"And why aren't these dishes done, young lady?"

"That's Nate's fault. It was his turn to dry, but he was late getting home, then Vinnie called."

*Yeah, right, Vinnie called her.*

"Enough excuses, Rebecca, get to it."

Becky lowered her eyes and went into her slumped, 'poor me' posture.

"Ah, Mom, Vinnie's waiting for me outside. We're meeting under the streetlight."

"When you finish the dishes, you can go see Vinnie, but it's already past six, and we eat at seven tonight, so only until then. And stay under the streetlight where I can see you."

She set the groceries on the counter by the refrigerator on the other side of the kitchen.

"In other words, Becky, the longer you sit there and whine, the less time you'll have with Vinnie."

"Ah, Mom, you're not fair."

Becky stood and slunk over to the sink.

Mom met her at the sink and hugged her. They were already the same height—five foot four—and wore the same size dress—trim or small or something like that.

"Just do your usual great job on these dishes, darling."

She kissed her cheek.

"You know you're my best helper, and I couldn't do the meals and everything else I have to do without you."

*I don't know about that, but if undeserved praise works to shut her up, I'm for it.*

"Hey, Nate!"

I turned to see Granddaddy facing me from the open garage door, the one on the right. Months ago, he'd fixed in place the one that swung open to the left. Light streamed from inside the garage and lighted his gaunt face and thin body. He went into a brief coughing spasm.

He wheezed, "Groceries!"

"Yes, sir. Coming."

I quickly checked Superman for ticks, pulled as much of the beggar's lice off him as I could see, then shut him in the pen. He trotted into his doghouse. After circling his bath mat a couple of times (a cotton, navy-blue mat I'd liberated from a neighbor's trash can weeks before), he crashed with his plump chin on his front paws and his weary, droopy eyes on me like, *Man, what a day!*

Granddaddy stepped into the garage and pulled the door shut behind him. I wanted to go to the garage window and see if I could tell what he was doing in there, but the groceries called. Plus, he usually kept the blinds closed, so I probably wouldn't have been able to see inside anyhow. And I wanted to be in the kitchen when Mom talked with Officer Lewis, so I hustled to the car.

Fifteen minutes after Mom's call, Officer Dan Lewis rolled quietly onto our driveway in his white Nash patrol car—no flashing red bubble gum machine, no siren. That was fine with me; I didn't want the whole neighborhood thinking we'd been robbed or something.

Lighted by our porch light, he strolled to our door wearing a gray fedora like Sergeant Friday on *Dragnet*. Instead of his uniform, he wore tan slacks, a white long-sleeve shirt, and a blue polka dot tie. I watched him from behind the living room window closest to the fireplace and wondered why he was dressed like a civilian.

Mom had been the desk clerk at the Southern Pines Police Department for over a year, so she knew Officer Lewis well. She told me he'd been a detective with the military police at Fort Bragg, North Carolina, just thirty miles east of us, then he got out of the Army six months ago and joined Mom and the others at the department.

Earlier I'd fed Superman and gotten back into the kitchen with the groceries just in time to hear her say over the phone, "Yes, Dan, I'm certain of it—Nate knows if he lies to me again, he'll be confined to quarters for the duration, so he's not lying this time. If he says there's a body out there in Barrow's woods, then there's a body in Barrow's woods."

From our sofa, which faced the front windows, Mom was reading when the doorbell chimed. She stood, dropped her *Woman's Day* magazine on our maple coffee table, straightened her dress, smoothed her hair, then met Officer Lewis at the door with a smile.

When he eased in, he looked about thirty years old, at least six feet tall, and maybe a few pounds overweight but still fit. He had always been behind a desk when I met him, so I was surprised that he looked that tall.

I stepped back from the window and stood beside Mom's antique rocker. The other window, the one closest to the door, held our first air conditioner, a six-month-old, big green Vornado unit with two air nozzles on the front that looked like they could be off a rocket ship. It may have been October, but in the sandhills of North Carolina, we still needed a little AC to sleep well. It hummed along at the lowest setting.

Lewis removed his Sergeant Friday fedora and revealed a tall forehead, light complexion, and close-cut red hair.

"Hi, Connie."

He turned to me, nodded, said, "Nate," then turned back to Mom and shook her offered hand. It wasn't polite for a man to offer his hand to a woman unless the woman offered her hand first. Mom had made that rule very clear to me years before—that and other rules of etiquette, like when walking with a girl, you walk on the street side of her, not the building side. That way, if a passing car splashed water or mud, it would hit you, not the girl. That was fine with me; girls were special, including Becky. But Becky was just a special pain.

Mom looked at me and held out her upturned hand toward Officer Lewis.

"Nate, meet the Southern Pines Police Department's first detective sergeant."

I think Detective Sergeant Lewis blushed a bit, but there were only a couple of table lamps on in the room, so I couldn't be sure. He looked at Mom, back at me, then used his thumb to push out the detective's badge he had clipped to his belt.

"Finished the six-week course in Raleigh two weeks ago, passed the exam this week. Feels good."

He smiled.

"But…lot of work to do, lot of back cases to work around here. He pointed his hat at me.

"Including yours, young man. You ready?"

I picked up the flashlight I had positioned on the maple end table by the rocker.

"Yes, sir, I'm ready."

I stepped toward the kitchen.

"Let me get Superman, and then I'll meet you at your patrol car."

I ran for the backdoor.

Behind me, Mom yelled, "Don't run in the house!"

I slowed in the dining room.

"Yes, ma'am! Sorry!"

I heard her laugh and say, "He's all boy, Dan."

Seconds later, leash in hand, I raised the horseshoe latch, then pulled the spring-loaded secret latch at the bottom of the pole (a Granddaddy invention) and opened the gate to the Superman Suite.

Superman raised his head and looked at me with snake eyes like, *The leash? Do you know what time it is?*

I snapped the leash onto his collar and half-dragged him out of his cozy cabin.

"Come on, Superman. Time to play police dog."

On my left side, he walked with me to the police car but kept looking up at me like, *But I don't want to play police dog; tell the nice officer to come back tomorrow.*

Detective Lewis stood behind the open driver's door with a microphone in his hand and asked into the mic, "Did he sign the search release?"

A raspy voice from the speaker inside the car said, "Wasn't happy about it, but he signed it."

"Ten-four. On our way. Meet you out front."

As I held the backdoor of the Nash open for Superman, I checked under the streetlight. No Becky, no Vinnie.

*Gee, what a surprise.*

Three minutes later, we did the turn-around in front of old man Barrow's dark, leaded-glass front door, then parked on the left side of the only other patrol car the police department owned. Both cars now faced the exit.

The whole house stood dark against a partly cloudy sky except for a yellowish light in one upstairs window.

I leaned forward and looked up. In that window and from behind the thin window curtains, a man's outline faced the drive. Then a left hand pulled one curtain aside. Leaning against the windowsill was the barrel of a rifle.

Chief Henry McDonald, the pot-bellied old man I recognized from a group Christmas party photo on my mother's dresser, snuffed a cigarette in his car's ashtray. He opened his door, limped the three steps to our car, and then put his left hand on the sill of my open window. The stench of a full, still-smoldering ashtray washed over me, not to mention the B.O. from his blue, food-stained uniform that looked like it hadn't been washed since WWII.

He pushed his police cap to the back of his head, leaned over, and spoke across my face.

"This better be for real, Lewis; we've got one unhappy voter in there."

He looked down at me.

"You got that, Nate?"

His breath smelled like roadkill on a hot July day. I choked down a gag.

"Yes, sir, I got it, but honest, Chief McDonald, there is a body—a man, and the man is dead with a hole in his head."

I pointed to the spot on my left temple where I'd seen the bullet hole.

"Right here."

He grunted.

"Yeah, okay, but why is that dog back there?"

Superman looked up at the chief and gave him a low tone, but not a full-blown growl.

"That's Superman, sir. He's the one who actually found the body. Part bloodhound."

He grunted again.

"Yeah, okay, okay. Drag that part bloodhound out here, and let's get on with it. Where do we start?"

I pointed back up the driveway.

"On the other side of the carriage house."

He looked up.

"That's a hundred yards away! Y'all can walk if you want. I'm driving."

Lewis slipped the strap of a Kodak camera with a flashbulb attached to it over his head, and then he held the camera to his chest as he got out of the car.

I joined him in front.

Under a break in the clouds that exposed the light of a quarter moon, Lewis, with Superman and me beside him, walked toward the carriage house. In a flash, a quick instant, a huge shadow glided between us and the moon, then poof!—it was gone.

*The shadow again!*

"Nate…"

I turned my eyes back to Lewis.

"Yes, sir?"

"Tell me everything you can remember. Start with why you

were on this property in the first place—that's trespassing, you know."

"Yes, sir, I guess it is, but we've always played in these woods, and nothing like this has ever happened before. And we're careful; we don't build fires or cut things down or anything like that."

"All that's fine and well, but it's still trespassing, so I recommend you find another place to play. Now…tell me why you were here and what happened."

So, I told him about the flying shadow (he said he didn't see it the minute before), my binoculars, Superman needing a walk (I kinda threw that in as an extra excuse), chasing Superman into the woods, then finding the body.

Meanwhile, moonlight reflected off the white sand mixed in with the clay of the driveway and showed us the way, like how Dorothy's yellow brick road showed her the way. After all, we were in the sandhills area of the state and—

"Nate, you with me?"

"Ah, yes, sir."

"Okay. You had binoculars, but did you happen to have a camera? Did you take a picture?"

"Ah, no, sir. I have a camera, but I didn't bring it. But even if I had, it was right at sunset and too dark and spooky in there to take a picture—and there were eyes on me! I just wanted to get the heck out of there."

"Eyes on you? What do you mean?"

"I don't know. That's just the way it felt."

We were past the carriage house now, and the chief's car, headlights blazing on high beams and casting our shadows the length of the driveway, cruised up behind us.

Beside me, Superman strutted along with his head high. After every few steps, he'd look up at Lewis and wag his tail, but Lewis didn't seem to notice.

When it felt right, I shielded my eyes and glanced back at the carriage house to get my bearings, then I flicked on my flashlight and shined it on the edge of the woods.

"It was right in here somewhere."

Lewis pulled a flashlight from his back pocket, a big silver one, like a foot long, and flicked it on.

A few steps later, I felt a tug on the leash. Superman, apparently now fully energized, had his nose to the ground and was headed for the trees.

"There's the rotten log I jumped! Here we go, Detective, hang on!"

A couple of minutes later, sweating and scratched, we popped out into the clearing where I'd seen the body. All three of us slowed to a walk. I scanned the area with my light while Lewis did the same with his. No lump on the ground and in the center…no dead body.

Lewis shined his light on the leaves and pine needles in the middle of the clearing and looked over at me.

"Here?"

"Yes, sir. Right here in the middle."

He circled the area with his light on the ground, then lowered the light to his side and looked at me.

"Well, Nate? I don't see anything—no body indentation, no blood...nothing."

I shrugged.

"Yes, sir, but I'm...I'm sure this is the place."

I pointed at the ground.

"The body was *right there*."

I felt a tug, and Superman led me across the clearing.

"I mean, look at Superman; he's still on the scent, but it stops here. He's as confused as we are."

Superman got about halfway to the edge of the clearing, sniffed something on the ground, then ate it.

I looked back at Lewis.

"Well, maybe not."

I couldn't see what the beast had consumed, but he'd obviously lost interest in the hunt, and his pit bull stomach had overridden his bloodhound nose. I blew out an exasperated breath and pulled him to me.

Lewis tapped his flashlight on his thigh.

"Well...no body, no crime, and I promised your mother I'd get you back home as soon as possible. You have papers to deliver in the morning, right?"

I nodded.

"Yes, sir."

"Okay, for the record, I'll take a couple of pictures, then you can lead us out of here."

A few minutes later, thanks to Superman's backtracking skills and the light from Chief McDonald's headlights glinting through the trees, we found our way back to the driveway.

The chief scowled at our report, then when I asked him if Mr. Barrow really looked like Boris Karloff, he slammed his fist on the steering wheel and drove off in a huff.

We got home a little after ten, and Becky wasn't there. Granddaddy was still in his workshop. While Mom and Detective Lewis talked by his patrol car, I put Superman away, showered, then brushed my teeth.

When Mom came back into the house, I kissed her cheek good night and then went to bed. But I couldn't sleep. Mom didn't even smile when I kissed her or offer to tuck me in, a long-standing Hawke family tradition. I left her sitting on the sofa, watching the front door with all the lights on, including the porch light. Sometimes I just wanted to strangle Becky.

As if worrying about Mom wasn't enough, I also kept going over the day's events, including the call from my distributor. He had a new customer for me, apparently a difficult one. He said he'd tell me about it when he dropped off my papers in the morning. So, I was still awake when I heard the front door open and Becky's voice in the living room. My alarm clock showed 11:15.

# CHAPTER 3
## CRIME MOVIE SERIOUS

At four o'clock the next morning, wearing jeans and a long-sleeve white shirt for visibility, I helped Mr. Glenn offload the pile of Saturday papers from the trunk of his weathered black Chevy. In the light from our front porch and the streetlight, we dropped them on the edge of our driveway.

With a cigarette dangling from the corner of his mouth and ashes all over his white shirt and blue slacks, he walked around to the passenger side, then pulled a clipboard from the seat. He shined his flashlight at an order form on the clipboard where he had circled an address with his pencil.

"You know where this is, right—660 Orchard Road?"

He jerked his thumb over his shoulder.

"Just behind those woods?"

"Yes, sir, that's ah, that's Mr. Barrow's address. The driveway is down a few houses."

"Correct. Here's the deal: Based on a phone conversation I had with him yesterday, he's been taking the Raleigh paper—

state capital and all that stuff, very interested in politics. But the *Raleigh News & Observer* has crossed him; they're supporting the wrong guy for governor, so he's decided to take our Charlotte paper and give it a try."

He took a copy of the order off the clipboard and handed it to me.

"Don't screw it up, Nate. Barrow is an influential guy around here; he owns the bank, the Chevy dealership, a big hunk of Aberdeen Mills, plus he's the city's mayor emeritus. Hell, his father helped start this town back in 1890. The old goat is retired now and reclusive but still powerful, and that's why I've been trying to get him with us for years. He can do us a lot of good if he's happy or do us a lot of harm if he's not."

I had no idea what a mayor emeritus was, but it sounded impressive.

He cleared his throat.

"Now, he wants the paper on the wrought iron table by the door handle side of the front door—rain or shine. Got that? Not in the yard or on the porch like the others. Understand?"

I nodded and looked out over the woods, still dark against the night sky.

"Yes, sir."

*Geez, why me?*

"I've already dropped off today's paper, so start with the Sunday paper tomorrow and collect on Friday with the rest."

"Yes, sir."

He grabbed my shoulder.

"Hey, don't look so glum. With Barrow signed up, you'll only need one more new customer to get that baseball bat I promised you."

*If I live that long.*

"Yes, sir, I'd like to have a bat."

"Then I'll see you in the morning with the Sunday papers."

He tossed the clipboard onto the passenger seat, then walked around to the driver's side. As he pulled the door open, he checked his watch.

"Gettin' late. Time to roll, wrap, and pedal."

I waved goodbye, then pulled the bag of rubber bands out of the pocket of my jeans and tossed it onto the pile. From the other pocket, I pulled out my Barlow jack knife. I took a knee, opened the blade, then cut the string from the papers.

*Yeah, "roll, wrap, and pedal." More like roll, wrap, pedal, and die on Boris Barrow's spooky porch. Geez.*

After rolling each paper, wrapping it with a rubber band, then packing it into the large wire basket in front of my bike's handlebars, I filled my Boy Scout backpack with the eight left over. I slipped into the pack with the pouch on my chest and the straps on my back. I checked to make sure I had my anti-mutt rocks in my front pocket and my slingshot in my back pocket, then I mounted my trusty red Schwinn Meteor. It was still dark, so I clicked on the flashlight I had taped to the basket and took off.

After an uneventful route, I rolled into our backyard at six-fifteen. For the first time in days, I wasn't attacked by the Lawsons' mutt on Connecticut Street or ambushed by Tom Ray Urdenbach, the career sixth grader and village bully. He sometimes got up early just to take a shot at me with his slingshot. Charlie had nicknamed him Turd-en-bach (but not to his face) after he saw his name on a school book as "T. Urdenbach." A day without Tom Ray was a good day.

Tom Ray was a weekly threat to me mainly because of collection day. When I'd gone by to collect the day before, he'd screamed through his screened door that he'd shoot me if I came any closer. The screen filtered my view, but I could tell he was holding either a real six-shooter or a cap pistol that looked like a six-shooter, so I backed off and decided I'd try again on Sunday when his mother was home. She operated a loom at the Aberdeen Mill, didn't make much money and was often a difficult collection, but she'd never pulled a gun on me. I'd never seen a father at the house.

I stuck my head in the backdoor, but the only sound I heard was the *tick-tock* of the clock on the kitchen wall above the table. Superman had heard me arrive in the backyard, so when I pulled my head back out and shut the door, he was awake and pacing at his gate like, *Come on, come on, gotta go, gotta go.*

While I filled his water bowl, I watched him mark every tree, bush, and fence post in the backyard. Then, after I'd given him a few pats and a good scratch behind his ears (he loved that), I put him away again.

Back inside, I heard someone in the bathroom. I changed to pajamas, fell into my twin bed, then slept until I felt a hand gently rock my shoulder. I smelled bacon. My alarm clock said 8:30.

"Nate."

Granddaddy turned his head and coughed.

"Fall out, young man, time for chow."

He returned to the kitchen, and I rolled out of bed thinking how lucky I was to have Granddaddy in my life. And how lucky I was to be healthy.

Mom had told me Granddaddy had been in the Army during World War I, "the Great War." He had been a sergeant in a bridging unit that got gassed with mustard gas by the Germans, and he hadn't been able to breathe well since. He didn't talk about the war that much, but when he did, I listened.

And he didn't let his damaged lungs keep him from working. After the war, he was a tool and die man with Chicago Steel up in Chicago. That's where he met his future wife on a trolley car ride to work in 1922. They married, then my mom was born, and then her brother. Mom was only six and in school when her mother and baby brother died in a gas explosion in their apartment building. Granddaddy had told the building supervisor that morning when he left for work that he thought he smelled gas in the building, but the supervisor didn't do anything about it in time.

With Granddaddy's brother, Uncle Albert, and his wife, Aunt Marion, taking care of Mom in Chicago, Granddaddy moved south to take a much better job in a washer and dryer manufacturing plant near Charlotte, North Carolina. It was also a much better climate for him than Chicago. He never remarried, but in a year, he was making enough money to bring Mom down to live with him and hire a very proper but sweet and loveable colored lady to take care of the house and watch Mom.

Then the Great Depression hit in 1929, and by 1932 Granddaddy and thirteen million other Americans had lost their job. Very few people could afford luxuries like a washer in 1932.

The colored lady became family, and even though her name was Hattie, she wanted to be known as "Mammy." So that's who she was—Mom's Mammy and, later, our Mammy.

Even during the Depression, when there were weeks without enough money to pay her, Mammy stayed on. Then finally, Granddaddy was able to get on with the WPA, a government program for out-of-work middle-aged men with families, and even though he may have been building roads, trails, and buildings in some national park somewhere away from Mom, he was able to send money home to Mom and Mammy.

After Mom married Dad and we were born, Mammy was

a grandmother to Becky and me, and boy, was she ever a stickler for manners and the proper use of the English language. We spent time with her and Granddaddy every summer and almost every Christmas, and I can still hear her say, "I don't want to hear any lazy tongues around this house. Use the proper word and enunciate it properly!"

And we did. Mom had taken us to Mammy's funeral in Charlotte in 1954, and then we brought Granddaddy home with us. That funeral was a sad and tear-filled occasion for all of us. I missed Mammy as much as I missed my dad.

After a bathroom call, I walked into the kitchen in my tennis shoes, jeans, and a blue plaid shirt.

Granddaddy stood over the stove wearing his favorite baggy Duke University sweatshirt and baggy jeans.

"What'll it be, Nate? Pancakes, eggs, or both?"

"All of the above, please; I'm starved."

I checked the kitchen table.

"No Becky? No Mom?"

"Your mom had to go to work this morning—lot of paperwork to get caught up on now that Officer...excuse me, *Detective* Lewis is back at work. And as for Becky...she's still asleep. She just grumbled, 'Go away' when I tried to wake her."

I sat at the side of the table against the wall and watched Granddaddy fork bacon onto my plate.

"What's with Becky, Granddaddy? Why is she so darn ornery and rude these days? I mean, she's never been Miss Positive Personality, but lately she's been downright evil."

"Well...I tell ya, Nate."

He scratched his head through his short gray hair.

"See, she's thirteen, almost fourteen—that's a tough age. She's dealing with hormones and puberty. Lot of changes are happening inside her body, changes that are affecting her both physically and emotionally. Hard times."

"I don't know what puberty or hormones are, but it doesn't sound like anything I want any part of."

With his face in the crook of his left arm and his head turned toward the backdoor, he went into another coughing spasm, then cleared his throat.

"I could tell you, but I'm not up to it right now, so I suggest you look in the dictionary or check with that set of encyclopedias in the living room."

He loaded the last egg onto my plate beside the bacon and pancakes, then walked toward the table holding his plate and mine. He smiled.

"To quote a Baptist preacher I once knew in Charlotte, 'It's in The Book.'"

"Okay, Granddaddy. I'll look it up."

He set the plate in front of me next to the napkin, knife, and fork.

"But you can't avoid it, Nate. Puberty will happen to you soon, probably in three or four years."

He nodded at me and winked.

"And I hope you handle it better than Becky."

He sat at the end of the table near the phone with a plate full of pancakes.

"Hey, I heard about you and Superman finding that body yesterday, so how are you going to top that today? There's a challenge, huh?"

He reached for the Aunt Jemima syrup.

"What's the plan?"

I wanted to bite into that bacon, but it wasn't polite to talk with food in your mouth, especially with others at the table, so I picked up the bacon and held it to my mouth to let him know I wanted to eat it.

"I plan to find that body again."

Just then, the phone rang.

Granddaddy leaned over and took the receiver off the hook.

"Hawke residence... Yes, he is, but he's eating breakfast right now... Okay, I'll tell him... Goodbye... That's okay, goodbye."

He hung up and looked at me.

"Call Charlie; he sounds all nervous about something."

He picked up his fork.

"And when you do, please remind him of basic phone manners."

He cut a slice out of his stack of pancakes and looked up at me with a steady gaze.

"Nate, I'm not crazy about the idea of you trespassing on Barrow's property again, but if you're serious about looking for that body and you do go on that property again, take Charlie with you. You'll need a witness."

With a mouth full of scrambled eggs, I nodded. (Can't talk with food in your mouth. But I think I've already mentioned that.)

"And you might also keep in mind that your mom talked with Detective Lewis last night after you came in. She tried to make your case, but the bottom line was that you are not to play detective.

"He told her, 'If—and to the chief and Lewis, that's a very big *if*'—there really was a body, it will turn up. Meanwhile, you are to do sixth-grader things and not police things."

He winked.

"But I didn't tell you that."

I swallowed and smiled.

"Yes, sir."

But then the smile faded like ice cream on a hot sidewalk.

"So, in other words, they don't believe me."

"Well, no, they don't. But in their defense, they only have your past record to go by. I doubt if they've forgotten that 'motorcycle gang' you saw robbing the Bank of Southern

Pines; the ones that were arrested then turned out to be two retired motorcycle cops on a road trip."

He chuckled.

"And they had just stopped to cash a check." He shook his head and took another bite of pancakes.

"Well…yes, sir, that was fun at the time, but that was months ago; I've matured since then. This time it's for real; somebody's been murdered. I'll show 'em, Granddaddy. There was a body, and I'll prove it!"

He swallowed. "I'm sure you will."

He sliced into the pile again, then studied it as if he was trying to decide if that slice, which was bigger than the last slice and soaked in even more syrup, was too big. Then he looked up.

"But just be careful, okay? You act more like your father every day, and sometimes that worries me."

I nodded. I had another bite of eggs in my mouth.

What Granddaddy had just said about my father didn't bother me. I knew he had liked and respected my father. He just didn't think a man with a family, which included his daughter, should take chances like my father did. But to my father, the Marine fighter pilot, there wasn't any other way to live.

I'd often overheard Granddaddy describe my father as "adventurous" and "reckless," and I understood why. I mean, his call sign was "Bingo" because he was always pushing the fuel limit of his F-9 fighter and barely getting back to his base or his carrier before he flamed out. "Bingo fuel" was the coded call to the base control tower for "Low on fuel, need priority clearance to land." My father had called "Bingo fuel" so many times that his squadron mates started calling him "Bingo Hawke." But bingo fuel wasn't what got him killed in Korea.

By the time we finished breakfast, it was nine o'clock, the earliest time of the morning to call someone on the weekend. Calls before nine were not permitted—bad manners—and dropping by someone's house before ten on the weekend was also rude, as was calling between six and seven in the evening, the usual supper hour. Mammy had really emphasized that one because meals were family time and not to be interrupted.

With my taste buds and stomach singing praise to Granddaddy for that breakfast, I stood at the counter and dialed Charlie's number.

As I finished dialing, Granddaddy put his hand on my shoulder and spoke into my ear.

"The dishes are soaking. Tell Becky pancakes are warming in the oven and not to forget to wash and dry the dishes before she goes out."

He smiled.

"I know it's not her day to wash, but hey, you snooze, you lose."

He gave me a gentle shake on my shoulder and then stepped for the backdoor.

The phone clicked. Charlie said, "Shonkasabe residence."

"Good morning, Horrible Charlie! What's the news over there at the Longhouse?"

Charlie had Osage and Creek Indian blood and referred to his large two-story house as "the Longhouse."

"Hey, don't call me that, okay? I mean, what if my parents heard you call me that? They'd think I'd done something really horrible."

"Well, to hear Rose tell it, you did! You pulled her precious blonde ponytail, Charlie. You should have known better than to mess with Queen Rose. So when she screamed, 'You're horrible, Charlie!' we were happy to bestow upon you that new title and only request that you wear it with pride and consider it a badge of honor."

"Well, I don't consider it a badge of honor!"

He paused and then laughed.

"Okay, maybe I do. I mean, she had it coming, telling on Chipper for passing me that note."

"She did have it coming, but you don't have to defend Mary Elizabeth Chippenvale, Charlie; Chipper can take care of herself. And did, as I recall. Didn't she wipe that mimeograph ink under Rose's desk top lid?"

"Yeah, it must have been her, and holy smokes, that was funny. Rose's fingertips are still blue. But hey, Nate, speaking of Chipper—and I'm sorry, but here comes your bad news for this Saturday—I saw her at the Five & Dime yesterday, and she wants to go to the movies with us this morning."

"What?"

"Yeah, her buddy Donna's gone to Durham for her grandmother's birthday. Chipper was even desperate enough to call Rose, but Rose is at some equestrian camp 'riding to the hounds' for the weekend."

"Charlie, no! That's going to put a major crimp in my plan today. You told her, 'No how, no way,' right?"

"Geez, Nate, I knew you weren't going to like this, but don't forget she's the cutest girl we know. I mean, you said yourself she looked like Annette Funicello. And she's smart, and... Well, heck, she's no flighty blabber-mouth like most of those girls. And you just said she could take care of herself, so don't sweat it; she can do whatever we do, and she can keep up. Besides, it's one of those old Humphrey Bogart crime flicks—*Key Latigo*, or something like that. Maybe she'll get bored and leave."

"In the first place, she may actually like crime movies, but in the second place, I'm not planning on going to the movies this morning. There's something more important I've got to do, Charlie, and I'll need your help. Come on, man, call her and tell her no."

"It's too late to call."

He sighed.

"She's shopping and then meeting us at your house at ten o'clock."

I shook my head and tried to think.

*Not good, not good at all.*

"Nate?"

"Yeah, yeah, I'm here."

"Well, what are we gonna do?"

"I don't know. Can you come over now?"

"Sure."

"Then beat feet over here, and maybe I'll think of something by the time you get here. Look, Charlie, I've got some stuff to tell you that you're not going to believe. Then you'll understand why we can't have Chipper in on this, and maybe you can help me figure out a way to get rid of her."

"This better be serious, Nate. I mean, we don't ever miss a Saturday movie."

"It's serious all right—crime movie serious."

"Oh. Okay, I'll throw a saddle on my pony and be on my way."

# CHAPTER 4
## THE PLAN

After I hung up, I opened the cabinet door under the counter, grabbed a few dog biscuits, then stepped toward the backdoor to get the leash. I thought I'd get in some training time with Superman before Charlie and Mary Elizabeth arrived. As I reached for the leash, I heard footsteps behind me.

"Where's my breakfast?"

I turned. Becky stood in the kitchen in her red striped pajamas and those gosh-awful yellow curlers in her hair. She yawned.

*How do they sleep in those things?*

Behind her, the radio in the bedroom she shared with Mom blasted "Sh-Boom," by The Crew-Cuts. Just as the Lone Ranger couldn't chase the bad guys without "The William Tell Overture" in the background, Becky couldn't spend a waking moment without rock and roll. Now don't get me wrong—I liked rock and roll too, especially "Sh-Boom," but I didn't need it every minute of every day.

I pointed at the stove.

"Granddaddy left you some pancakes warming in the oven."

"Great…pancakes again. You'd think that old wheezer-geezer would use his imagination sometimes and fix something more edible than pancakes."

"Pancakes were the only things that would keep in the oven until Your Highness awakened, my dear ungrateful sister."

"Oh, shut up!"

She stepped up to the oven and grabbed the oven mitt.

"And he told me to tell you to wash the dishes when you're finished."

She spun around.

"I'm not washin' the stinkin' dishes! It's your stinkin' turn!"

"It's your turn now; he said so."

"Well, I'm not washin' the stinkin' dishes, and that's all there is to it!"

I leaned against the counter and crossed my arms.

"What's with this *stinkin'* stuff? You've never used that word before."

She opened the oven door.

"Kids used *stinkin'* in the movie, *The Blackboard Jungle*. It's a good expression. Vinnie uses it; it's cool."

She pulled out the plate of pancakes and set it on a trivet on the counter.

"Vinnie's seen it, and he wants to take me to see it."

"*Cool*, huh?"

"Yeah, *cool*, you square, you ignorant know-nothing child who makes up stories about finding a body in a clearing!"

She walked toward the kitchen table with plate in hand.

"And how is Vinnie going to take you to see it? You walking? Riding bikes?"

She stopped and looked at me with the dreaded Bossy Becky Squinted Eye.

"He was sixteen this week, got his license, his dad bought him a new car, a red and white '55 Chevy convertible with a really cool red and white interior, and I'm goin' to see that movie with him!"

"A new car? What the heck does his father do?"

"He's the vice president of the Pudgy Pig chain, two hundred and eighteen stores."

"Well, how come I've never seen him? Seems like a guy with that much money would cast a bigger shadow."

"He's too important to leave New Jersey, that's why."

"And his mother? She's here, right?"

"When she's not at the Pinehurst Country Club playing bridge."

She jabbed a finger at me.

"Just shut up, okay? It's none of your stinkin' business!"

"Okay, okay. Hey!"

I nodded at the stove.

"You didn't turn off the oven."

She slammed her plate down on the table.

"You turn it off, smart guy! It's bad enough I'm grounded, but now I have to put up with your stinkin' comments! Get outta my life!"

I bounced off the counter and reached for the leash.

"I just wish I could, oh how I wish I could."

I opened the door just as a pancake went splat against the wall by my head.

*Well, better than a plate.*

I stepped out but paused and stuck my head back in the door.

"Good luck going to the movies if you're grounded."

She snapped her head around.

"You'll see!"

Outside, the humid morning air lingered, like summer wasn't ready to give up on the sandhills just yet. From the garage workshop, I heard a sporadic metal-on-metal clang. I opened the gate and stepped into the Superman Suite. He stood and wagged his tail like, *Where we goin', where we goin'?*

I hooked him up to the leash.

"It's training time, Superman."

He made a low guttural sound like, "Huruhhh?"

"Yes, training; as in I give commands, and you obey them. We'll start with a remedial course in the ever-popular 'Sit.'"

I held up a dog biscuit, then put it back in my shirt pocket.

"That's the prize, okay?"

Two minutes and a dozen "Sit" commands later, with the leash in my left hand and Superman still standing by my left side, I knelt beside him and lifted his floppy ear.

"Superman...no sit, no dog biscuit. You copy that?"

Superman looked over at the driveway and let out a happy yelp.

Mary Elizabeth, wearing bib overalls over a white shirt, slid her bike around the corner of the house and stopped. She hopped to the ground, knocked the kickstand into place with the toe of her black-and-white saddle oxford, then brushed her short, curly, dark-brown hair back with her fingers.

"Hey, Nate! Am I on time?"

"Hey, Mary Elizabeth. Yeah, I guess. Charlie's not here yet, so I've just been trying to teach Superman how to sit."

She stopped in front of Superman and put her hands on her hips. Below her dark and prominent Annette Funicello eyebrows, her brown eyes narrowed.

"What kind of dog is this?"

I looked at Superman.

"He's the stubborn kind."

She put a hand to her chin.

"Short, mostly tan hair, wrinkled skin, floppy ears, and a wide stance. I'd say bloodhound with a dash of bull terrier."

I looked up at her and smiled.

"Hey, that's pretty good. You know dogs?"

"Hounds mostly. My grandparents had fox hounds. We

have a spaniel now. They're retriever dogs, but we don't use Sofie for bird hunting and retrieving. She's just a house dog."

She held out her hand.

"May I try?"

I handed the leash to her.

Superman quick-stepped over to Chipper. He stood in front of her with his head up, tongue out, tail wagging, and an adoring gaze in his goofy eyes.

She glanced at Superman, then looked at me.

"Do you have any treats?"

"Just these."

I handed her a dog biscuit.

"Oh, that'll do fine. Now, where would you like to begin with this pupil, Nate? 'Sit'?"

"Yeah, 'Sit.' And good luck."

"Okay."

She positioned Superman on her left side with the leash tight, looked down at him, showed him the dog biscuit, then, in a firm voice, said, "Superman...sit."

Good ol' Superman just looked up at her and stared like, *You sure are cute.*

She laughed.

"Okay, I get it—need some encouragement, don't you?"

With a grin, she glanced at me and then back to Superman.

"Superman...sit."

At the same time she said, "sit," she switched the leash to

her right hand but kept it tight to keep his head up, then pushed his rump down to the ground with her left hand.

She let go, and he stood up again.

I frowned and shook my head.

She repeated the cycle three times with the push. Then on the fourth, with her left hand by her side this time, he miraculously and finally sat on her command.

She gave him the dog biscuit and hugged him with a background of "Good dog, Superman, good dog!"

He ate it up—the praise, I mean. Well, actually both the biscuit and the praise.

She handed the leash to me.

Just as I had Superman in position on my left side, Charlie, wearing a red North Carolina State T-shirt (his father's school) and jeans, wheeled around the corner and slid to a stop beside Chipper's bike.

Up to then, I'd never seen Chipper in anything other than a school dress, so until the time of her arrival, I'd planned to tell her that hanging out with us that day wasn't going to be any fun; we weren't going to the movies; we were going to the library. I did have a couple of *Hardy Boys* books to return, so that wasn't going to be too much of a stretch. But after I saw how she was dressed, how she handled her bike, and how she handled Superman, I decided she really could be part of what I had in mind.

Charlie walked toward us with a serious look on his tanned

face and his warrior-like shoulders slumped. As he walked, he brushed his long, dark-brown hair out of his eyes and over his ears. Charlie had the longest hair in the sixth grade by a long shot and wore it parted down the middle. That led to some occasional grief from our principal, but it never got long enough to cover his ears, so he got away with it. He pulled on his hawk-like nose, then shrugged.

"Hey, you guys. Sorry I'm late, but I had a flat tire, the road was flooded, got pulled over by the cops, stung by a bee…just a really bad morning."

I pointed at him.

"You had to watch *Winky Dink*, didn't you?"

He threw his shoulders back, and his face brightened.

"Well yeah, Nate! I knew you'd understand. I just got my magic screen yesterday, special crayons and all, so I couldn't miss this morning's show, could I?"

He looked over at Chipper.

"You understand, don't you, Mary Elizabeth? You're the forgive-and-forget type, right?"

"I didn't plan this powwow, Charlie, so don't look at me."

I took a knee beside Superman and looked up at Charlie.

"Okay, you're forgiven. Just cool it a minute, and I'll fill you in."

I unhooked Superman from the leash so he could run around, then I led Chipper and Charlie over to one of the only two trees we had in our backyard—a tall long-needle pine that stood back by the wire fence. We sometimes played in the woods on the other side of the fence, but those woods were only a few yards deep and formed the back edge of a yard belonging to a big colonial house and people I'd never seen.

In the shade of the pine tree and out of hearing range of Becky, I told them about finding the body and—

Charlie held up his hand at me like a traffic cop and said in his deep Tonto voice, "Whoa there, Kemosabe. You find body?"

He swallowed.

"You find dead man?"

"That's right—a very stiff, dead man."

Chipper blew out a soft whistle.

"Wow, Nate, what'd you do? Did you know who he was? What was he wearing?"

*Just like a girl to want to know what he was wearing.*

"Slacks, shirt, and tie. And no, I didn't know who he was. Now, let me finish."

I went on to tell them about contacting the police, how the police didn't believe me, but how they went back to the scene with me last night anyhow, how the body was missing, and how they really didn't believe me then. Finally, I wanted to go back to the scene today to see if I could find any clues that would help convince the police I wasn't lying.

Charlie looked at Chipper and put his hands on his hips.

"Well, now. You still want to hang around with us today, Mary Elizabeth?"

She glanced from Charlie to me.

"You're darn right I do! Let's go!"

# CHAPTER 5
## THREE IN HARM'S WAY

As the three of us walked down the driveway toward the street, I glanced back at the house. Becky stood in the front bedroom window in a black dress. No curlers, hair combed. She watched us with her arms crossed, chin high, and cheeks drawn back in a cruel half-smile. The effect reminded me of the Evil Queen in *Snow White and the Seven Dwarfs*, like Becky was up to something or knew something the dwarfs didn't know. We dwarfs pressed on, this dwarf (call me Doc) with the strap of his box camera around his neck.

I had decided to leave the less-than-obedient Superman behind. I felt sure I could find the clearing without him, and I didn't want him barking and alerting old man Barrow or anyone else. If I couldn't find the clearing on my own, I had Charlie, the Osage/Creek Indian tracker, as a backup. I also had a paper sack inside my shirt for evidence, and in the back pockets of my jeans, I had my slingshot and a Sherlock Holmes-type magnifying glass from my science kit.

Finding the clearing again turned out to be easy. On Charlie's advice, all I had to do was follow the broken twigs and trampled bushes and vines. Fortunately, none of those vines were poison oak. Either that or I wasn't sensitive to poison oak. But I wasn't going to rub any on me to test that theory.

The circular clearing looked larger in the daylight—about seven or eight yards across with only a few tufts of grass growing through a bed of dried leaves, large pine cones, and pine needles. Overhead a canopy of oak and pine limbs filtered the sun, leaving only a few rays of sunlight illuminating spots on the ground. I stepped into the clearing and pointed at a tuft of grass in the center.

"He was right there on his right side with his knees drawn up."

Charlie walked up on my left, and Chipper walked up on my right. Charlie stepped past me, bent down, and examined the tuft of grass. He looked up at me.

"Something has been here, Nate. The grass has rebounded, but most of the blades show signs of stress like they were bent at one time. And recently."

"Okay, that fits."

I pulled out my sack, pinched off a few of the bent blades of grass Charlie showed me, then bagged them. I also bagged a few of the leaves around the grass.

I stood and made a sweeping motion with my hands.

"Look, let's spread out, and each of us take a section of the area. Look for anything that doesn't belong here and especially anything that looks like blood. I'll start here where we came in."

Charlie walked ahead and then bent down. He picked up a big oak leaf and showed it to us.

"My *witsiko*—my grandfather—taught me a long time ago that when tracking, look for limbs and leaves that have been disturbed. If you see a limb or leaf that looks like it's been here a while but not in the position it's in now, turn it over and check for blood on the other side."

We nodded.

Chipper walked toward the right side of the clearing and scanned the ground with each gentle step. She stopped and raised her head.

"Hey, Charlie, if we pick up every leaf that looks like it's been disturbed, we'll be here all day. Just look at this place; it looks like a herd of goats has been through here."

Charlie stood erect.

"You know what? I was just thinking the same thing. There have been a lot more people here than just Nate and Detective Lewis."

"Well, sure," I said. "Whoever brought the body was here, and whoever moved the body was here."

I pointed at the right side where Chipper had kneeled in one of those sunbeams to examine something.

"We were never over there, Mary Elizabeth, so whatever

disturbance you find there was not caused by us. We just came up to the center of the clearing where the body had been, circled it, then went back out the same way."

I grimaced.

"Well, there was Superman; he wandered around here a bit."

Charlie stepped around the edge of his section and said as if talking to himself, "Someone had to bring the body here, and someone had to take the body away."

He looked up.

"How big was this guy, Nate?"

"Heck, I don't know; he was all curled up on the ground. But he wasn't small. He was a full-grown adult."

I shrugged.

"But he wasn't extra tall or extra heavy either."

"Well, it still sounds like it might have taken two guys to move him."

Chipper stood from a squat, the sunbeam highlighting her curly hair.

"Hey, take a look at this. This sure doesn't belong here."

She turned to us and held up a blue fountain pen with a gold clip.

I threw up my hand.

"Don't move."

I took a careful step her way.

"Put a rock or stack of pine cones or something to mark

where you found it. Oh, and don't put more fingerprints on it than you already have."

"No problem, Nate. I'll wrap it in my hankie."

She pulled a white handkerchief from the bib of her overalls, then looked up at me and must have noticed my raised eyebrows. She grinned.

"Hey, I watch *Dragnet* too, you know."

I grinned back at her. Then I saw an egg-size rock on the ground and picked it up.

"Here, you can mark the spot with this."

I tossed it to her. She caught it in midair with one hand.

*Geez, maybe Charlie's right; maybe she can do anything we can do.*

A few minutes later, I had decided we weren't going to find anything else when Charlie hollered, "Hey, you guys!"

From the far edge of the clearing, he took a knee, bent over, and reached to the ground. Then he straightened his back, turned, and held up something small and yellow.

"Candy corn!"

"Now I know what Superman was eating over there! Mark it, Charlie. See any more?"

He scanned around him, turning over leaves and twigs.

"Nothing. If there was more, maybe Superman ate it."

Chipper chuckled.

"Does that mean the dead guy had a sweet tooth?"

Charlie shrugged.

"Or the killers did."

I studied where Charlie had used a large pine cone to mark the location of the candy corn. The night before, Superman had stopped to nibble whatever he'd found before he would have gotten to that mark. My eyes widened when I also realized those two spots were generally in a line from the damaged tuft of grass in the center. I stepped back to a few feet behind the center and raised my arm to show the line.

Charlie noticed and stood.

"Are you saying that's it—someone came in or went out on that line?"

"Yep, I think so. From the center of the clearing to where I saw Superman eat something off the ground to your pine cone is a straight line."

He pointed toward Chipper's rock.

"And I'll bet that pen fell out of the body's pocket, or the pocket of someone carrying the body, when it came in or went out that way. If we follow a line from the center of the clearing where the body was, to that rock and beyond or to my pine cone and beyond, that will lead us to the body."

I nodded.

"That makes sense, but which line seems to be the most likely one to follow?"

He turned and looked at the area outside the clearing on his line.

Chipper did the same on her side, then looked at us.

"Hey, you guys. Someone has gone out or come in from over here. Look for yourselves."

Charlie had stepped up to a gap in the woods between the trunk of a small oak and the limbs of a small dogwood.

"Someone has been this way too."

He turned to us and held a thin broken branch from the dogwood in his hand.

"And it looks like they were coming into the clearing, not out. Hang on, and I'll take a look over there."

I met Charlie on the right edge of the clearing where Chipper leaned over to me and whispered, "Is the game afoot, Holmes."

I raised my eyebrows and mimed holding a pipe.

"Yes, Doctor Watson, I believe it is. Quite."

Charlie visually checked a line from the center of the clearing to the rock, then took a few steps into the woods between two pine saplings. A few steps later, now past a tall pine, he bent down and pointed at a couple of large pine cones.

"Crushed, both of them, and disturbed, and from the direction of where they had been to where they are now, I'd say this is where the body was carried out."

He stood and pointed in the wide general direction of the big house and the carriage house.

"That way."

I took a step.

"Well, let's go."

Charlie held up his hand and shook his head.

"No, Nate. Wait a minute."

He scratched the back of his neck.

"What about this? You stay here. Stand behind the center and eyeball it for me; keep me lined up, and I'll go ahead. I might be able to read the trail they made. You know, just in case they didn't go in a straight line."

Chipper and I said in unison, "Good idea, Charlie."

We looked at each other, then all three of us laughed. Man, that was weird.

So that's what we did, and sure enough, twenty yards from the clearing, Charlie curved to the right and more toward the driveway. At that point, we didn't need the lineup, so Chipper and I weaved between the trees toward him. But then he froze in mid-stride, turned, waved at us like we were about to fall off a cliff, then held one finger to his lips.

We stopped, but he waved us on with his left hand while holding up his finger. We tiptoed on as silently as we could— Chipper leading, me guarding the rear, like the Sioux sneaking up on Custer.

When we reached him, he pointed ahead, in the direction he faced. I followed the line of his arm and finger and there, barely visible through the trees, was the weathered and overgrown back wall of the two-story carriage house.

I whispered, "The trail goes to the carriage house?"

Charlie nodded.

"Straight to it. The trail curved for a bit, then at this point, where the carriage house is visible, it straightens out and aims right at it."

Chipper stuck her head in between us.

"So that's where they took the body?"

Charlie shrugged.

"Looks that way. Let's go."

A few minutes later, we stood where the trail ended—right at an old wooden barrel that sat against the carriage house wall and under a large, open, second-story window. Tall, thick blackberry bushes lined the wall next to the barrel. Above, the old wooden shutter to the left side of the window dangled by the top hinge. The other shutter lay among the blackberry bushes and Virginia creeper vines to the right of the barrel, its hinges and screws frozen in rust. Overhead, tall oak limbs shaded us and reached out over the roof.

Chipper and I stood on the right side of the barrel where someone else had already trampled the bushes. And recently.

Chipper's eyes widened. She pointed at the window.

"Up there?"

We nodded.

Charlie gestured that he would get on the barrel first, then I should go and stand on his shoulders. That plan made sense because Charlie was thicker and heavier than me and had that tall, sturdy Osage build that impressed Lewis and Clark when they traveled through Osage territory in 1804. I'd read a book about that back in June. I gave him a thumbs up.

While Charlie got into position on the barrel, I noticed a few faded and warped boards above the barrel were scratched, like someone's shoe had tried to get traction against them. I tapped Charlie on his leg and pointed to the scratches. He nodded.

Chipper grabbed my arm and whispered.

"Maybe this would be a good time to call the police."

"Trust me; they wouldn't believe us. We still don't have a body."

She raised her eyebrows and looked up at the carriage house window.

"But what if the killers are in there?"

"Well, good point, but I don't think they would have hung around after ditching the body, and all the signs suggest they ditched the body here."

She sighed.

"I hope you're right."

I handed her my camera.

"Hold this for me. If I need it after I get up there, hand it to Charlie, and he can toss it to me."

Charlie extended his hand, then grabbed my wrist as I grabbed his, the way we were taught in Boy Scouts. Then he pulled me up, first to the top of the barrel, then he helped me climb onto his bent knee. He squatted even lower while I braced against the wall and put one foot, then the other, on his shoulders.

When he stood erect, it was like riding an elevator right to the sill of the window. I put my hands over the sill and raised my head just enough to peer in. Very dark, very quiet. From a tree or maybe the sky behind me, a crow cawed. A gust of humid wind rustled the trees. Oak leaves bounced off me, and in the sky above, a shelf of dark gray clouds slid between us and the sun. I lowered my head and looked down to my right.

Charlie stared up at me.

"See anything in there?"

I looked back inside, my eyes more adjusted to the darkness that time, then back down at Charlie.

"Very dark, but it looks like this was a hayloft; the floor is right at the bottom of the window. No dead body, at least not that I can see. Some old wagon wheels, broken furniture, newspapers. Need to get inside to see more."

"Okay."

All of a sudden, Charlie grabbed the soles of my tennis shoes. I looked down. He bent his knees, stood, extended his thick arms, and shot me into the window.

With a thud, I landed on my chest and arms and lay in a cloud of dust, my feet and ankles sticking straight out over the windowsill and my shins in pain from the impact.

*If someone is in here and didn't hear that, they are deaf!*

I raised to my hands and knees. As the dust settled and

my eyes adjusted, I saw that the loft only extended about ten feet. Beyond and below was a two-story open space with horse stalls along the ground-level wall and two old horse carriages in the middle, one for two people and one for six, probably the station wagon of its day. I could tell by footprints in the dust around me that someone else had been there recently, but I still couldn't see a body.

I pulled in my feet and turned around.

Outside and below me, Charlie looked up. "Well?"

"I still don't see a body. But if the body is here, it could be downstairs or hidden among the junk in this loft. I just don't see it."

Charlie turned to Chipper.

"You wanna go up and help him look?"

She rubbed her palms on her hips, glanced left, then right, and generally didn't look ready to be the next person launched through the window.

"You wanna wait down here for us?"

"No...no."

While she was making up her mind, I glanced at the pile of old newspapers nearest to me. I blew away the dust on the top paper, which read *Barrow Against Unions*. I scanned a few more. They all dealt with the textile union movement and were all dated 1929.

I looked back over the window sill at Charlie.

Charlie looked at Chipper.

"Well, make up your mind, girl, time's-a-wastin'."

She took a breath and grabbed Charlie's wrist.

He got her off the ground and onto his shoulders the same way he'd done with me, then she stood and leaned her hands against the wall. Charlie held her ankles and stood erect.

She looked up at me.

I extended my hand.

"You gonna pull me up?"

"Unless you want the catapult treatment like he gave me."

She turned to her left and looked down at Charlie.

"Now go slow, Charlie, I…."

She sucked in a breath and let rip a piercing shriek that could have been heard at the soda shop on Broad Street.

She nodded toward the ground like her head was a dribbling basketball.

"There, Charlie, to your left, between the bushes and the wall!"

About three feet from the barrel, at the base of the wall and hidden from view by overhanging vines and blackberry bush limbs, I could barely make out gray slacks, white shirt, and a lump that looked like my friend the body.

"Holy smokes, Charlie, it's him! Get me down from here!"

A shot rang out and a bullet hit the carriage house.

Dust jumped off the window frame around me.

"Geez! He's shooting at us! Look out, Charlie, here I come!"

Chipper slid down Charlie's back onto the barrel's edge, then jumped to the ground.

I spun around, slid over the windowsill, and hung there by my hands.

Charlie grabbed my hips and dropped me onto the barrel, then both of us jumped to the ground.

With me in the lead, followed by Chipper, then Charlie pulling up the rear, we took off around the side of the carriage house closest to my street, then burst out onto the driveway at full gallop.

I looked back, and Chipper was right on my butt.

*Man! She can catch and she can run fast!*

Fifteen seconds later, we hit the street and I slowed to a walk, breathing hard, sweat pooling in my eyebrows.

Chipper slowed to a walk beside me, then Charlie joined us—both sucking air. I put my hands behind my head, pulled in a deep breath, then wiped the sweat from my eyebrows with the sleeves of my shirt.

*Finally, I have witnesses. They've got to believe me now!*

After we caught our breath, we jogged for my house and the telephone. It wasn't until we got into the house that I realized…no camera.

# CHAPTER 6
## BAD NEWS

We walked straight to the phone in the kitchen, where I pointed at the refrigerator.

"There's usually a pitcher of cold water in the fridge and maybe some lemonade. Help yourselves."

I stopped at the far counter, reached up, and opened a cabinet door.

"Glasses here."

I picked up the phone and took a glance around the kitchen. Dirty dishes filled the sink, and the "oven hot" light still glowed on the stove.

"And Charlie, turn off that oven for me please."

"Got it. Where's Becky? Kinda nice not having her in here harassing us."

I dialed the number I had memorized.

"If the radio's not on, she's not here."

Chipper reached into the cabinet and took down three tall glasses.

"Southern Pines Police, Mrs. Hawke."

I made a fist.

*Yes!*

"Mom, Mom, I found the body again! And old man Barrow shot at us!"

"What? He shot at you? Nate, are you all right?"

"Yes, ma'am, I'm fine; the bullet just hit a wall."

"Hit a wall? What wall? Nate, where were you?"

I grimaced.

"Well...I was in the loft of the carriage house."

"Well, no wonder he shot at you—you were trespassing on his property!"

"I know, Mom, but I found the body!"

Behind me, Charlie cleared his throat.

"That is, Charlie, Mary Elizabeth, and I found the body. I've got witnesses, Mom!"

She sighed.

"Oh, Nathan, what am I going to do with you?"

"Mom, just tell Detective Lewis I found the body again, okay? Please? Please just tell him to hurry up and get over here."

"Oh, I don't know, Nate. He's really, really busy. We're the only two here today, and he's at his desk in his office with a stack of files piled up to his chin."

"Well, is Officer Lum on duty, maybe on patrol or something?"

"No, it's Saturday, and he and the chief are off today."

"Well, can you get away? Mom, please, I need someone—anyone—to come over here so I can prove I wasn't lying!"

She sighed again.

"Oh, Nate... Okay. I'll see if I can get Dan to take a break and come over. If not, I'll try to get away for a few minutes myself."

"Great! Thanks, Mom. And the body is right behind the carriage house—easy to get to, so it will only take a minute."

"Well, we'll have to call Mr. Barrow to get his permission. We can't get a search warrant today."

I let out a breath.

"Oh, yeah...permission."

"Nate, are you sure Mr. Barrow shot at you?"

"I heard a shot, and a bullet hit the wall near me. I know he has a rifle; I saw it in his window last night when we were over there."

"Well, okay... Let me speak to Becky."

"Ah..."

*Dad-gum-it, Becky!*

"She can't come to the phone right now, Mom."

"Okay, then have her call me. And Nate..."

"Yes, ma'am."

"It's eleven-thirty-five, so maybe, if Mr. Barrow agrees, I can run over there during lunch."

*Uh-oh.*

"Well, okay, but we could meet you there, and I could make you a sandwich and bring it with me."

"No, I've got my lunch here. I'll just pick you up and run you over there with me. Then I'll scoot back here and eat at my desk."

"Ah....at noon?"

"Yes, noon—if Mr. Barrow agrees. I'll let you know one way or the other by... Well, as soon I know if he agrees or not."

"Geez, thank you, Mom. Thank you, thank you."

She chuckled.

"You're welcome, sweetie. Talk with you in a few minutes."

"Bye, Mom."

We sat at the kitchen table and sipped our glasses of cold water. Unfortunately, there wasn't any more lemonade; I suspected Granddaddy.

I took the evidence bag out of my shirt and put it in the empty chair. Then I watched the clock on the wall while Horrible Charlie and Chipper laughed over the retelling of the Rose and the ponytail incident. Chipper confirmed she was the one who put the mimeograph ink under Rose's desktop.

Then, at 11:58, the phone rang. To a background of chuckles from Charlie and Chipper, I jumped up from the kitchen table and grabbed it after the first ring.

"Mom?"

"Nate, that's not how I taught you to answer the phone."

"Yes, ma'am. Sorry, Mom."

"Okay, try it again."

"Hawke residence, Nathan speaking."

"That's better."

"Are you coming, Mom? Are you coming?"

"No, I've decided to stay here and work over lunch so I can leave early this afternoon."

I threw my head back and sat down at the table.

"But Dan is on his way and will be there in a few minutes."

I straightened.

"Thanks, Mom, thank you."

"And, Nate... I went to bat for you with Dan so tell me again... Are you *certain* you saw a body?"

"Yes, ma'am, the body is there, I'm certain."

Charlie leaned over toward the phone.

"It was there, Mrs. Hawke; I saw it."

Chipper leaned over from her seat against the wall.

"I saw it too, Mrs. Hawke."

"Well, okay. Dan's coming because he thinks it will be best if he talks with Mr. Barrow instead of me. Plus, if the body is there, he'll need to do the right things to safeguard the body and the area as a crime scene. And he'll have to get the coroner out there."

"Yes, ma'am, I understand. We'll be in our driveway waiting for him."

"Okay, sweetie. Bye for now. I'll see you later this afternoon."

"Bye, Mom."

I hung up and turned to the others.

"Detective Lewis is on his way and will meet us out front."

Charlie made a fist.

"Great."

Chipper smiled at the news but then lowered her head.

"I'm sorry I left the camera, Nate. I put it on the ground just before Charlie pulled me up, but in the excitement...."

"Hey, it's okay. I can be a forgive-and-forget type too, you know. I'll get the camera when I go back with Lewis."

She set her glass on the table, slid out of her seat, and stood.

"Well, I've got to get home for lunch."

She walked toward the backdoor, then turned and smiled.

"But this has been fun; you boys sure know how to show a girl a good time."

Charlie and I laughed as I walked over to open the backdoor for her. I mean, guys open doors for girls; that's just the polite thing to do. I opened the door.

"Anytime, Mary Elizabeth."

She brushed past me, then stopped in the doorway and turned.

"Will you call me and tell me what happens with the police?"

*Call her? Call a girl?*

"Well…"

"Or I could come back later, and you could tell me about it then."

Charlie stood and walked toward us.

"Yeah, come on back, Mary Elizabeth. We'll give you all the gory details then. Heck, we may have this case solved by this afternoon."

I glared at him.

He noticed and shrugged.

"Or not. I guess it would be best if we called you first. You know, just in case."

"Okay, call me as soon as you know something. After all, I'm on this case too, you know."

She stepped onto the step.

"Oh! Two things."

She turned. She reached into the bib of her overalls and pulled out the pen wrapped in the handkerchief.

"Don't forget this."

She handed it to me.

"And don't forget my party Monday night—eight o'clock. Wear a mask but no costume, and be ready to rock and roll!"

She waved, then stepped into the yard.

From his sundeck, Superman gave her another happy yelp.

"Hi ya, Superman! You should have been there, you smart dog. It was great!"

As Chipper's kickstand clanked, I shut the door and looked at Charlie.

"Be ready to rock and roll? Dance, Charlie? We're going to have to dance?"

"Yeah, I'm afraid so. It was in the invitation. Didn't you read it?"

"I did, but maybe I just blocked out that part."

I sighed.

"Not good, not looking forward to that."

I gestured toward the front door.

"Well, come on, Charlie. Throw down your drink and let's go meet the cavalry."

"I'm ready, but first... You got anything to eat on the way? I'm hungry."

I opened the cupboard by the fridge and took out the graham crackers.

"These do?"

"If you got peanut butter to go with them."

"No time."

I tossed a sleeve of crackers to him and headed for the front door.

"Come on, time for a photo op with that itini...itini-something corpse. What's that word we had in class?"

"Itinerant? Moves around?"

"Yeah, itinerant. Time for a photo op with that itinerant corpse."

I led Charlie to the front door, where we stepped out and stood on the stoop. A minute later, Detective Lewis wheeled the white Nash patrol car onto our driveway. The blackwall tires crunched to a stop, and he killed the engine. He looked at us like he'd just heard a friend had died and rested his arm on the windowsill.

We jogged over to him.

As I pulled up, he tilted his fedora to the back of his head.

"I'm sorry, Nate. Mr. Barrow is in no mood for company today."

"But Detective Lewis...the body, what about the body?"

"He says there isn't a body, there never was a body, and not only that, but he never took a shot at you. He said he never heard a shot either."

He shrugged.

"That's all I can do, Nate. On Monday, we can get a warrant and try again, but that's not likely; the judge is a friend of Mr. Barrow. Plus, I talked with the chief before I came over here, and he's fuming to the point of yelling at me. You gotta understand, Nate. The chief is up for reelection, and Barrow's support is critical."

He turned the key in the ignition, and the car rumbled to life.

"So, sit tight until Monday, and I'll get back with you then."

Standing on my right side, Charlie bit into a graham cracker with a loud, angry crunch.

Lewis looked at Charlie and tilted his head back as if he hadn't noticed him.

"Oh, sorry, Detective Lewis."

I held out my hand to Charlie.

"I'd like to introduce you to my friend, Charles Shonkasabe."

(That's another etiquette thing my mother and Mammy drummed into me; you introduce the older person to the younger person first, then the younger to the older. Also, you introduce the females to the males first.)

I gestured to Lewis.

"Charlie, this is Detective Lewis."

Charlie, stone-faced, gave Lewis a slight head nod.

Lewis smiled.

"Oh, yeah, I've seen you around town, Charles. Nice to meet you. Hey, you weren't named after Charles Brent Curtis by any chance, were you?"

Charlie's eyes narrowed like *How did you know that?*

"Well, yes, sir. I was."

"Well, Charles, judging by your broad shoulders and who you were named after, you must have some Osage blood. Charles Curtis was Osage and the first Native American to be vice president of the United States. I know I'm going to sound like a book nerd here, but I love history and I believe I've read he was vice president in 1929 under Herbert Hoover."

Charlie, now relaxed, nodded.

"My great-grandfather was Osage, my great-grandmother was Creek and a former slave to a Cherokee master, so, yes, sir, I have Osage blood."

"Well, I'll bet those great-grandparents had fascinating lives. I've got to get back to work, but I'd like to hear about them."

He shifted the shifter on the column up to reverse.

"Come down to the SPPD sometime, and let's talk."

He pointed at me.

"And bring this character with you. The Cokes are on me."

Lewis turned to look over his right shoulder and the engine accelerated, but before he let out the clutch, I grabbed his arm.

"Wait!"

He turned, and the engine went back to idle.

"Yeah, Nate?"

I reached into my pocket and pulled out the pen wrapped in the handkerchief.

"Here."

I handed it to him.

"We found this in the clearing this morning where the body was lying yesterday evening."

He held the handkerchief in the palm of his left hand. The

cap of the blue pen with the gold clip stuck out from a fold. With his right hand, he shifted down to neutral.

"A fountain pen? You found this where you found the body?"

"No, sir. We found it on the edge of the clearing where I found the body. It was on a line from the center of the clearing where I'd seen the body to where the body had been taken. That's how we knew which direction to go to find the body again. Then Charlie tracked it, or the people carrying it, all the way to the carriage house."

He looked up at me.

"Very impressive, Nate."

He looked over at Charlie.

"Very impressive, Charles."

Charlie smiled.

"Thank you, sir. But you can call me Charlie if you like."

"Okay, I will. Good job, Nate and Charlie, good job."

He picked up an envelope from the passenger side of his bench seat, then slid the pen off the handkerchief and into the envelope.

"You'll want this handkerchief back, right, Nate?"

He held it to his nose.

"Smells like there might have been a young lady involved in this caper."

He handed it to me.

"Well, yes, sir. There was."

"Well, my congratulations to her as well. Okay, now I've really got to get back. You guys come on down sometime for that Coke."

He put the Nash in reverse again, then looked over his shoulder and backed out of the driveway. In the street, he shifted again, then as he turned the car toward town, he waved and we waved back.

Charlie looked at me.

"Well, now what?"

He snapped off another bite of his graham cracker.

"I don't know, but I sure would like to take a picture of that body. Anything could happen before Monday."

I glanced at the woods.

"Maybe we could take the foot trail by the streetlight and come up to the carriage house from the woods. Even if someone saw us on the trail, they wouldn't know what we were up to."

I looked up at the tall and puffy dark clouds that had gathered around us.

"Then again, I thought I heard thunder a minute ago."

I considered that a second.

"Ah, heck with it. Rain or no rain, let's go back."

Charlie stepped in front of me and held up his hands.

"Easy there, big fella, hold your horses. Now that we're back in the land of peanut butter, couldn't we discuss this over lunch? Say...with a little Campbell's chicken soup?"

A heavy raindrop splattered on his nose. Another hit me on the shoulder, then I looked up and got one in the eye. I pushed him on the arm.

"Charlie, I think it's lunchtime."

As we jogged for the front door, rain splattered around us and thunder boomed in the distance.

"But when the rain stops, I'm going after my camera and another shot at that corpse!"

# CHAPTER 7
## GRANDDADDY'S SECRET

J ust as we cruised into the kitchen, the phone rang. Mrs. Shonkasabe was on the line and wanted her son to get home between the raindrops; something about lunch was waiting. Actually, she said, "At the next break in the rain."

A few minutes later, before I had Granddaddy's glass humidifier filled and Charlie had finished slathering the peanut butter on our last graham cracker, the rain stopped. Now that Charlie had to get home to feed at the family trough, it occurred to me I could use the break in the rain to sneak over to the carriage house, get my camera, and photograph the corpse. But there was Granddaddy, and he needed my help.

Charlie stuffed the last of the cracker in his mouth, opened the backdoor, and yelled a garbled, "Hi-yo, Silver!"

He leaped out and closed the door but stuck his head back in a second later.

"Hey, Nate, How come Tonto never said, 'Hi-yo, Scout?'"

I looked up from the sink.

"That, my friend and faithful companion, is one of the

mysteries of the old west. I have never understood that myself."

"Me neither."

He ducked out and closed the door.

When the humidifier was full, I moved it to the counter just as the backdoor swung open and Granddaddy wheezed in. He didn't sound good, and when I turned around, he didn't look good—sunken cheeks, stooped shoulders, and a pale and frail frame inside that Duke sweatshirt. It looked bigger on him than ever.

"Granddaddy, why don't you let me heat some soup and fix us a sandwich?"

He stopped in the middle of the kitchen and coughed abruptly into the crook of his arm.

"Phew, I guess soup would be a good start, but I'm ready for a hamburger and potatoes, something to stick to my scrawny ribs."

He coughed again, then blew out an exasperated breath.

"I'm okay. I just need to hang around that humidifier for a while."

He made a cavalry charge gesture with his arm and stepped for the hallway.

"But first…to the bathroom!"

By the time he got back, I had the tomato soup heating on the stove and the hamburger patties laid out on tin foil the way he liked it: Two patties ready for his secret seasoning and the foil ready to catch the extra rosemary, thyme, and oregano spices. Meanwhile, the humidifier finally spewed steam.

With a white hand towel draped over his head, he went straight to the humidifier and leaned over it so the towel would catch the vapors. He coughed, then looked at me.

"My project is coming along, Nate, and it's time I brought you into my devilish scheme."

He took two deep breaths.

I stood beside him on his right side and stirred the soup, which already showed heat waves.

"Are you sure I'm old enough to learn of your 'devilish scheme,' Granddaddy? Sounds dangerous."

From under the towel, I heard a chuckle.

"You're old enough. It's not that devilish or dangerous. It's just that I need your help."

He took another deep breath, then lifted his head and looked at me with the towel hanging over his brow and ears like one of those wigged British judges I'd seen in my history book.

"Do you know what an iron lung is?"

"I think so. Something to do with polio, right?"

He leaned over the humidifier again.

"That's right. Children with polio can't breathe; the muscles in their lungs don't function anymore, so they have to lay inside this big steel cylinder from the neck down. Then the cyclic pumping of the iron lung pushes air in and pulls air out of their lungs. It keeps them alive, but they can't leave the iron lung. Not ever. Very depressing sight. And that's why you and your classmates got the polio vaccine this year."

He turned his head and coughed.

"Thank goodness Dr. Salk came up with that. It saved a lot of children."

I opened the cabinet door above the counter and reached for two soup bowls.

"Soup's ready."

I set the bowls on the counter.

"Crackers?"

"Ah…yeah, graham crackers would be good. With peanut butter?"

He lifted his head and smiled at me.

"Sound good to you?"

"Sounds great to me, but we're ah…we're a little short of graham crackers right now. How about Ritz?"

I stepped around to the other cabinet.

"You okay with Ritz and peanut butter?"

He put his face back over the humidifier.

"Sure, any cracker with peanut butter will do, Ritz, saltines, whatever."

A few minutes later, the hamburger patties were in the oven, and Granddaddy and I sat at the kitchen table inhaling the vapors from the tomato soup and dipping our spoons to the back edge of the bowl. That was another rule: You spoon and scoop soup to the back of the bowl and not toward you and the front of the bowl. As Mammy used to say, "You don't lap it up like a dog."

And at all costs, you do not slurp. Very rude to make any noises with your food or drink.

After a few spoonfuls of that warm, sweet tomato soup, I looked across the table at him.

"Granddaddy, would an iron lung help you?"

I waited and took a drink of milk while he finished a bite of a Ritz sandwich with peanut butter.

He swallowed.

"Well, I sure hope so because I have one sitting in the garage that I've been repairing for weeks. It better work."

"Really? In our garage?"

"Yep. It's an old clunker the hospital had replaced with a newer model a few years ago. It would never be used again and was just collecting dust and taking up space, so I asked about it.

"The materials manager, who is also a veteran and a good friend since I started working there, told me he'd be glad to get rid of it, so if I wanted it, I could have it.

"So, I got another friend from the hospital to help me; he's the guy who runs the Maintenance Department the two days of the week I'm off. You've heard me talk about Fat Pat, the guy who lives at the bowling alley in his spare time, right?"

I'd just taken a bite of cracker, so I nodded.

"Well, Fat Pat and I, plus the four strong orderlies I hired, picked a day when you kids were in school, and your mom was at work, and we got that beast home in Pat's pickup. Then we stored it in the garage."

He shook his head.

"That monster is heavy! Good thing I took the motor and pump out first, or we couldn't have done it."

"Well, how can I help?"

"I've finished overhauling the pump and motor, so in the next day or two, I'll be ready to reinstall them. I'll need your muscle then. After that, I'll need your help to get me in and out of that thing and crank it up for me."

He scooped another spoonful of soup but held it over the bowl.

"I don't think I'll need to use it every day. I just want it for rough days and special occasions, like the occasion I'm planning for Becky."

He spooned the soup into his mouth and swallowed.

"According to Dr. Pettifog, the pulmonary specialist, or lung doctor, I saw at the Salisbury VA in March, recent research says the iron lung has helped veterans with damaged lungs like mine."

"So, what's the occasion?"

He scooped and swallowed another spoonful.

"Her birthday."

"That's only, what, a week away?"

"A week and a day, so I need to get that beast up and running."

My soup had cooled enough by then that I could just scoop it up without having to blow on every spoonful, so I finished it off. Granddaddy did the same. I stood, reached for his bowl, and then took our bowls to the sink. I turned.

"So what are you going to do for her birthday? Or is that the confidential part?"

"Well, I told you about the iron lung in confidence; not even your mother knows about that. But I also told you I have plans for her birthday. Let's keep both of those things to ourselves, okay?"

"Well, sure, Granddaddy, I can keep a secret. What's the plan?"

He stood, went to the humidifier again, then draped the towel over his head.

"I want to take her out for a dinner date, just the two of us, down to The Holiday restaurant on Broad Street. I want to show her how worthy she is of a male's respect and demonstrate to her how a man should treat a woman one on one. So, to be able to do that without embarrassing her with my wheezing and coughing, I'll need to be able to breathe good for at least an hour."

"Oh, well yeah, that makes sense."

I reached into the bread box on the counter and took out a couple of hamburger buns.

Granddaddy straightened up long enough to put oil in the skillet, dump in the potatoes I'd sliced, sprinkle them with salt and pepper, then turn on the burner. He turned to look over his shoulder at me.

"Nate, your father was a good man, but he didn't know what to do with a daughter. In his world, it wasn't manly to have a girl. So, he just left the parenting of Becky up to your mother. And that's okay as far as it goes, but a girl needs a daddy or at least an adult male figure like an uncle or granddaddy who can fill the role of a good daddy.

"In my opinion, and the psychologist at the VA agrees, a young girl needs to hear positive comments like, 'You look really cute in that dress,' or 'That hairstyle is perfect for you.' And she particularly needs them from a male figure she respects and who respects her and wants only the best for her.

"In fact, I believe she gets her self-worth, her value as a female, from such a male figure. Anyhow, when you came along, your father ignored Becky even more and concentrated on you, the first-born son, the son who gave him status among his peers."

He stirred the potatoes.

"Not your fault, Nate, of course, but I think that explains why she gives you such a hard time. It's resentment. And then, to make it worse, your dad was killed in Korea just as Becky turned eleven, a time when she needed his love and compliments the most."

He set the spatula on the edge of the skillet, then flipped the towel over his head again and leaned over the humidifier.

"She simply doesn't like herself."

"Geez, I had no idea."

I stepped to the refrigerator to take out the mustard, ketchup, and pickle relish.

"So you think that's why she's hanging out with that greaseball Vinnie?"

"That's exactly what I'm thinking. I've seen them together under the streetlight with him sucking on a cigarette and heard them on the porch with him making fun of everything she says. She just doesn't value herself enough to see him for who and what he is. And with her low self-esteem, she's going to keep choosing boys and eventually a husband who doesn't value her."

"So that's why I want to do my best to be a good daddy substitute for her on her special day. I want to show her how worthy she is of a good man and a good man's respect."

He cleared his throat.

"And with the help of that iron lung, I want to keep doing that for her for a long time to come."

He took another deep breath.

"I just hope it's not too late."

He raised and looked at me.

"And by the way, Sherlock, what happened today? Did you and Charlie find that body?"

So, I told him what had happened; how we tracked the body, got in the loft but no body, found the body, then got shot at, and how old man Barrow refused to let Detective Lewis on his property.

When I finished, he shook his head.

"Sounds like Barrow is either a very bad shot or just wanted to scare you off. And it also sounds like he's hiding something."

He turned and hung his head over the humidifier.

"Do you think he shot the guy, and if so, why?"

"Yes, sir, I think he shot him. I mean, the hole in the guy's head was a small hole and not a gaping hole like from a shotgun, so I think he used the rifle I saw leaning against the windowsill last night. But as to why, I have no idea. Hopefully, it wasn't because he was trespassing."

I opened the refrigerator and reached for a tomato.

"But the most puzzling part to me is the lack of blood."

He raised a bit and took another deep breath.

"No blood, huh? Sounds like he was shot somewhere else and moved to where you found him."

I set the tomato on a plate and picked up a carving knife.

"Which raises another question: How could one old man move a full-grown adult body by himself?"

"Yeah…that doesn't fit."

He coughed a quieter cough than usual, then cleared his throat and leaned back over the humidifier.

"So now what? If Lewis can't do anything, do you let it drop?"

Outside the kitchen window by the backdoor, lightning flashed. A second later, thunder shook the windowpanes. I glanced up just as a sheet of heavy rain pounded against the glass. I turned back to Granddaddy.

"I can't just let it drop, Granddaddy. After we dine on your hamburgers and fried potatoes…."

I pulled the oven door down and checked the hamburgers—done, with nice crispy edges.

"And assuming we get another break in the rain, I'm going back over there to take a picture of that body before it disappears again."

He chuckled.

"Sorry, Nate. Can't hear you—humidifier's too loud."

# CHAPTER 8
## LET THAT DOG LIE

The rain didn't let up, so I did my math homework. Between trips to the humidifier, Granddaddy watched TV. Neither of us mentioned Becky's absence.

At three o'clock, Granddaddy cut off the TV and returned to his workshop under our orange and blue umbrella. I put away his humidifier. Even though I knew Granddaddy would disapprove, I also washed and dried the dishes. He had already talked to me several times about covering for Becky. He called it "enabling."

I looked it up, and he was probably right. But I felt sure Becky would figure she was already grounded, so what else could Mom do? Then she'd let the dishes soak in the sink as a symbol of protest against Mom's unfairness. Then Mom would come home after work, see the dishes, and be upset. I was tired of seeing Mom upset.

I put the dishes away, and then it was time to see what I could learn from the evidence I'd collected. As I reached for my evidence bag on the kitchen chair, I heard the front door open.

I grabbed the bag and walked into the dining room in time to see Becky—black dress soaked, hair dripping water like a drowned rat—enter the bedroom she shared with Mom. A trail of water led from the front door.

Through the window in the door, I saw a red and white convertible with the top down. It backed out of our driveway and into the street. Vinnie, who looked like a greasy drowned rat, held the steering wheel with one casual hand. His soaking wet buddy, "Bones" Meecham, sat in the passenger seat and wiped the rain from his skinny face. Vinnie shifted gears, then drove off in the rain down toward his house.

I smiled. It looked like somebody didn't know how to put up the top on their hot new Chevy.

I walked up to the bedroom door and knocked.

"Becky, you okay?"

"Go away!"

"You need anything? Towels?"

"I need you to get the hell out of my life! Now!"

*Uh-oh, four-letter words. Mammy is turning over in her grave and looking for a switch.*

"Okay, I'll be in my room. Don't forget Mom is working today, and it's Saturday, so she may be home early."

"Go away, damn it, go!"

"Okay, okay, I'm gone."

I stepped over to the room I shared with Granddaddy, entered, and closed the door loud enough for her to hear it. She needed towels, and she'd have to go past my room to get them. I stood behind my door and listened. A few seconds later, I heard squishy footsteps go by me and into the bathroom.

I walked to the other side of my room, then sat at the maple desk under the window. I switched on the bronze desk lamp in the center of the desk and pulled my science kit microscope closer to me. I'd never used it to look for blood before. Usually, Charlie and I just examined flies, or bugs, or boogers. Sometimes we used the glass slides with the kit to examine snot. That was neat; snot looked like a sheet of ice under the microscope.

I emptied the sack onto the desktop and carefully spread the contents. There were three large oak leaves, a few pine needles, and five blades of grass. The grass and needles didn't seem to hold any clues, but one oak leaf showed promise.

I slid it under the microscope and focused on three circular-shaped spots. The largest spot, reddish and about the size of a penny, was fuzzy and probably mold. The second spot was brown, had ragged edges, and was half the size of the mold spot. It looked like it could be eggs from some kind of bug. The third spot was much smaller and black. I focused tighter. It reflected the light as glossy black and lay against a vein in the leaf as a thick and near-perfect circular spot, but my scope didn't have the power to reveal any more details.

I looked up and stared out the rain-streaked window. On *Dragnet* or *Sherlock Holmes* or one of those crime shows, dried blood was described as black, glossy black. And the bullet hole in the body's head had been black. I stood to get a separate sack for that leaf.

As I opened my door, Becky walked into the kitchen. With a blue towel wrapped around her head and her pink bathrobe flowing out behind her, she looked like one of those characters in the movie I'd seen a couple of years ago called *Aladdin and His Lamp*. Patricia Medina played Jasmine. I always thought Medina was a looker, but Rita Hayworth was my favorite. Mom looked like Rita when Rita had brown hair.

Becky went straight to the laundry room door on the far wall between the counter and the kitchen table. When she turned to open the door, she moved a bundle wrapped in a soggy white towel to her right arm.

I went straight to the cabinet under the counter where we kept the empty paper sacks.

Without a word between us, I returned to my room, but on the way, I heard water rushing into the washing machine.

After I put the leaf with the black spot into its own sack and the other evidence back into the original sack, I heard the door to Becky's bedroom close. Then car tires rolled up our driveway and past my bedroom window.

I jogged to Becky's door and knocked.

"Becky, Mom just drove up."

"Get lost."

I scoffed.

"I hear and obey, Princess, and meanwhile, may the fleas of a thousand camels roost in your navel orifice."

Then I noticed the trail of water drops from the front door again.

"And may your soggy trail of tears from the front door go unnoticed by the Queen."

Becky shot out of her room with her wet hair flying and the blue towel in her hand.

"Get outta my way!"

As she passed, I splayed my body against the wall, then stepped toward my room. I'd done all the enabling I was going to do for one day, but then I stopped. I decided I wanted to see what news Mom had from the SPPD, so I walked back to the kitchen to head her off and give Becky more time to compose herself.

Through the kitchen window, I saw Mom, in a floral print dress, hold her purse on her head and run through the raindrops toward the backdoor. When she hit the step, I opened the door and held out a clean dish towel.

She entered, grabbed the towel, then wiped her face.

"Phew, thank you, Nate. What a day to get caught in the soup."

She wiped her arms, then looked around the kitchen.

"Oh, thank goodness Becky did the dishes. I sure wasn't

looking forward to going another couple of rounds with her today."

She cocked an ear toward the laundry room.

"And she's doing a load of wash. How 'bout that?"

I shut the door.

*Yeah, how 'bout that.*

She pointed at me.

"And you, young man, what have you been up to?"

"I've been playing crime-scene investigator with my science kit."

She walked toward the kitchen table.

"And? Find anything?"

"Maybe a blood spot, but I couldn't tell for sure. You suppose Detective Lewis could identify it for me?"

She placed her purse on the table and sat at the end near the phone.

"I suppose so."

She bent over and wiped her legs.

"I think he would need to send it to the crime lab in Raleigh for a positive ID and a full report, but I'm sure he could give you an educated opinion."

She looked up.

"But not today. He's been whittling down that pile of back cases, and he's beat."

She smiled.

"I gave him the rest of the day off."

"Anything new on my case?"

"Not that I know of. No mention of it at the office."

"Oh. Okay."

I glanced at the refrigerator.

"Mom, you need anything to eat or drink? We don't have any more lemonade, but there's cold water and milk."

"Oh, yeah, milk and graham crackers would be good. Thanks."

I squeezed my lips together and shook my head.

"Well, Mom, about those graham crackers...."

She grinned.

"Charlie's been here."

"Yes, ma'am. 'Fraid so."

I stepped for the cabinets.

"But we've got Ritz or saltines."

She stood.

"I'll get something, Nate, maybe cheese and saltines with milk. You can go back to your evidence room if you like."

I stopped in front of the refrigerator.

"Well, at least let me get your milk."

She stepped over to the cabinet with the glasses.

"Okay, what is it?"

"What's what?"

"You're stalling, Nate. What's on your mind?"

"Ah, well, there is something on my mind, but I don't want

it on my mind, and I don't want to do what I've got to do to get it off my mind."

I took the half-gallon milk carton out of the refrigerator and set it on the counter.

"It's about a girl."

She brought over a glass from the cabinet.

"A girl, huh? Well, no wonder you're stalling. Who is this lucky lady that is occupying your preteen mind?"

"Mary Elizabeth."

"Oh. I like her."

"Well, I like her too, but the problem is she's having a Halloween party on Halloween. That's Monday, Mom, only two days away, and she told Charlie and me to be ready to 'rock and roll.' I'm afraid that means dancing. I'm not even twelve yet. What do I know about dancing?"

She stepped over to me and hugged my shoulders.

"First, thank you for reminding me of Halloween. I'll pick up some treats at The Pig on my way home tomorrow, probably suckers. Second, maybe it's time we did something about your social skills. Tell you what… After my snack, let's go into the living room, and I'll teach you some basic dance steps. I doubt the girls will expect any of you guys to be Fred Astaire, so the basics will do."

She sighed and glanced off into space.

"You know, your dad and I liked to dance—swing, rumba, waltz. We even won a prize one time—a pig."

She looked at me.

"Can you believe it? The prize was a live pig! That was at some crazy squadron party at Cherry Point."

She rolled her eyes.

"Crazy Marines. Well, needless to say, we passed on the live pig, so I guess the lieutenants took it back to the farm they stole it from. Who knows?"

By then, I had the milk poured and the cheese out, and she had the saltines on a plate. We moved to the kitchen table. She went back to her original seat, and I sat at the opposite end.

"You know, Nate, I taught all this dancing stuff to Becky last year. Maybe she'll join us for a refresher course."

I waved my hand.

"No, Mom, please. Becky's been in one of her moods today so let's just let that dog lie."

"I heard that!"

Behind me, Becky entered the kitchen and slapped me on the back of my head.

"I'll lay you out; then we can let *you* lie."

Mom stood.

"Rebecca Louise! Just when I was feeling all warm and fuzzy because you had done such a good job on the dishes, you come in here and start something."

Becky glanced at the sink.

"Oh, yeah, well… I was told to do it, so I did."

Mom pointed at her.

"Now, tell your brother you're sorry."

Becky gave me a cursory glance.

"Sorry."

I smiled and cleared my throat.

"Apology accepted, Princess."

Mom sat and said, "That's better."

She crossed her arms and stared at Becky's attire—hair in curlers, pajamas, and robe.

"Are you just getting up?"

Becky opened the refrigerator.

"What's to get up for? I'm grounded."

"Don't get smart with me, Rebecca. I asked you a civil question, and I expect a civil answer. Are you just getting up?"

"Yes."

"Yes, what?"

From inside the refrigerator and as if speaking to a head of lettuce, Becky said, "Yes, ma'am."

Mom shook her head and blew out a breath.

I decided I'd done all I could to keep Becky from ruining Mom's day. It was time to get out of the line of fire.

"Mom, let me know when you're ready to rock and roll. I'll be in my room looking for dancing shoes."

She took a bite of her saltine and cheese sandwich and nodded.

But Mom never called me for dance class that day. Later, I heard her in the kitchen talking with Granddaddy, and

I thought she was crying. I figured her day had been long enough, so I let it drop. I wanted to help her, but I couldn't think of anything I could do short of strangling Becky. Mom probably would have considered that a little extreme, so I let it go.

Later that day, I let Superman out to chase a few squirrels and run around in the rain while I stood guard under the umbrella. Mom was home, so going back to look for the body and find my camera was no longer an option. I focused on the next morning—Barrow's paper, collecting from Tom Ray's mother, Lawsons' mutt. Hopefully, by the end of the next day, there wouldn't be two of us crying.

# CHAPTER 9
## THE THIRD FIGURE

At four-thirty Sunday morning, I stepped onto our wet stoop and closed the door. The rain-soaked front yard and driveway glistened under the brilliant stars that filled the night sky from horizon to horizon. A crisp breeze hit me, so I snugged down my blue ball cap and pulled up the collar on my windbreaker. Mr. Glenn arrived, and I met him at his car with my pocket knife and a plan.

The Sunday papers came with a stack of advertising inserts, so they had to be unwrapped and inserted into each paper before the paper was folded and banded. That took time, plus the papers were so big and heavy that it took two trips on my bike to get all of them delivered. I had saved the Barrow and Tom Ray papers for daylight, so they came last.

With the route done and those last two papers in my wire basket, I pedaled down the street under a bright blue sunrise, then turned left onto Barrow's driveway. But the delivery had to come second. First, I planned to find my camera and take a picture of that corpse.

When I got to the carriage house, I pulled over to stay out of sight of the house. I propped my bike against a pine tree on the edge of the woods, listened to make sure I was alone, then held my nose in case the body had gotten ripe. I crept around to the back. At the barrel, I stopped and searched the ground…no camera, no body. I released my nose.

Shaking my head, I ambled back to my bike, saddled up, then pedaled down the drive.

As I approached the house, I noticed a two-car garage directly in front of me on the other side of the turn-around. I hadn't seen that in the dark on Friday night. It faced the turn-around and was built in the same stone and style as the big house, but it didn't look as old. Between the garage and the end of the house ran a trim, three-row garden of green vegetables. Shovels, a hoe, a wheelbarrow, and other tools lay against the garage wall.

I slid to a stop in front of the stone steps to Mr. Barrow's porch and kicked my kickstand into place. As advertised, a wrought iron table sat on the porch just to the right of the leaded-glass front door. With paper in hand, I jogged up the steps. As I leaned forward and extended the paper over the table's edge, the front door opened with a metallic creak. I popped to attention.

The door opened wider, and a deep voice from the dark entryway said, "Young man?"

I pulled the paper back, held it in front of me, and looked

up as an extremely large human being dressed like a penguin stepped into the doorway.

"Sir?"

From behind him, a male voice with a slight tremor said, "Who is it, Wickers?"

Wickers, tall, thick, and bald with a bent nose, looked like he'd been one of those TV wrestlers who had lost a few grudge matches to Gorgeous George, Mighty Jumbo, or one of the other TV wrestlers Granddaddy watched every Sunday afternoon. Wickers glanced back into the house.

"A young man, sir. Your paperboy, I believe, sir."

"What'd you say? Speak up, Wickers, please."

Wickers stood even taller and projected.

"A young man, sir. Your paperboy."

"Ah. Show him in, Wickers, show him in."

"Very good, sir."

Wickers looked down at me.

"Please come in, young man. Mr. Barrow would like a word. And bring the paper with you."

With eyes wide and feet on alert, I stepped through the door onto a marble foyer and smelled cigar smoke. I glanced up at the wood-paneled ceiling high above me. It had a reddish tint and looked like the mahogany-beamed ceilings I'd seen on the cover of one of Mom's *Better Homes and Gardens* magazines. A wide staircase to my left with marble steps and polished wood railings along a stone wall apparently led to the second floor. Ornate rugs hung from the walls, and a bronze statue in medieval chainmail and sword guarded the approach to a sitting area. I felt like I had entered King Arthur's castle.

Wickers held out his hand.

"May I?"

I looked at his hand and then at my paper.

"Oh, the paper." I held it out. "Yes, sir."

The shaky voice said, "Over here, young man."

Just beyond the guard and standing in front of a crackling fire in a fireplace large enough to hold our car, an elderly man in a maroon velvet robe and leather slippers held out his hand.

"Come over here, please."

He curled his fingers to wave me forward.

"I apologize for the fire as it may be too warm for you, but at my age, I need warmth. I promise I won't keep you."

I walked over to him with cautious steps, like the marble floor of the foyer, and then the polished wood floor of the sitting area was a minefield. But when I got up close, you know what? He really did look like Boris Karloff, right down to his thick eyebrows, deep-set eyes, and pointed chin—at least a Boris Karloff with gray hair and a gray mustache.

He leaned on the cane in his right hand and looked over my shoulder.

"You may go, Wickers."

"Very good, sir."

Wickers placed the paper next to a dimly lit tiffany lamp

on an ornate wooden end table. The table sat between a stuffed leather rocker and a matching leather chair. All three pieces faced the fireplace while a cigar stub smoldered in the ashtray on the table. Wickers picked up the ashtray and drifted out of the room.

"Young man, your name is Nathan Hawke. Is that correct?"

"Yes, sir, Mr. Barrow, but you may call me Nate."

He smiled weakly.

"Very well then, Nate."

He cleared his throat.

"Nate, I invited you in this morning because I wanted to tell you how delighted I am that you will be our paperboy. You see…"

He leaned toward me and winked.

"I have a good view of my property from my widow's walk as well as my bedroom window, so I have observed you from afar as it were, and in so doing, I've become quite aware of your propensity to spend time in my woods."

He stood straighter, or at least as straight as he could.

"During those observations, you struck me as a very resourceful and enterprising young man, a young man not unlike myself when I was your age. I am specifically referring to your recent crime-scene investigation."

*Uh-oh.* I swallowed.

"Nate, it is said that all press is good press even when it's bad press, but I don't subscribe to that. Therefore, I would like to clear up this issue of the corpse in my woods as quickly and quietly as possible. I do not want any press of any kind, especially bad press. Do you understand?"

He took a step back from the fire and held out his hand as if to suggest I do the same, which I did, happily. I could already feel the sweat running from my armpits and the glow on my cheeks.

"Yes, sir, no press. I understand."

"Then I suggest we work together on this *case*, if you will. In other words, I'll tell you what I know; you tell me what you know, then maybe we can clear this up together."

I nodded.

"Very good."

He cleared his throat again.

"Nate, other than you and your friends, I have recently seen figures in the woods on two occasions. They weren't children playing Robin Hood or some other game like you and your friends do. They seemed to be engaged in something serious. Now, mind you, this was in the daylight. I'm not sure what else was going on at night. Also, last night after I spoke with Detective Lewis, Wickers informed me that he heard a shot on my property yesterday and may have heard another shot last Friday afternoon."

He pointed to his ears and shrugged.

"I didn't hear any of that, you see. How does that measure up with your investigation?"

I swallowed as best I could and took another half step away from the fire.

"I found the body in a small clearing near the center of the woods late Friday afternoon, sir. Then it was moved sometime later because it wasn't there when Detective Lewis and I looked for it Friday night. My friends and I found it again Saturday morning by the carriage house. I was going to take a picture of it, but then a shot scared us off."

"You wanted to photograph a dead man, Nate?"

"Yes, sir, but only to prove I wasn't lying about the body in the first place. When I reported it to the police, no one believed me. Except my mother, but she's my mother so...."

"Yes, I quite understand. Now, Nate...this body. Can you describe it for me?"

"Yes, sir. Adult, wavy blond hair—kinda like a movie star—gray slacks, white shirt, blue tie, and he was lying in a fetal position."

He reached up and stroked the gray mustache above his thin lips.

"And blood?"

"No blood other than what was on the shirt and in the hole in his head."

"Oh, so my clearing wasn't the crime scene."

"No, sir. I believe the body was moved there after the crime was committed."

"Well, that's good."

He took a deep breath.

"So far, so good, Nate. And what happened yesterday morning when you wanted to take a photograph?"

"After we got shot at, we took off and forgot the camera, so I never did get a picture."

"Well, to ease your mind, that wasn't Wickers or me who fired that shot."

"Yes, sir, I realize that now."

He smiled.

"I don't think I could even hit the carriage house from here with my little rifle. It's a pellet gun, you see, and I only use it to chase rabbits out of my garden. I can't hit them either."

I smiled back at him and shrugged.

"Well, any idea who did fire that shot?"

"I'd say somebody who didn't want you to photograph that body."

"Yes, sir, that's for sure. Did you see anyone on your property after that shot ran us off?"

"It rained all afternoon yesterday, as I recall, and I do enjoy watching it rain from my front porch, but I was in my bedroom when I saw them yesterday. I have tea in my room in the afternoon, you see, and I'd just finished my tea and was watching it rain from my window. That would have been, oh…midafternoon, say between three and four o'clock."

"Yes, sir, well, somebody moved the body between eleven-thirty yesterday morning and this morning because I checked on my way over here with your paper, and the body was gone again. So, that could have been what they were doing when you saw them from your window."

I scratched behind my ear.

"So, you saw figures on two different occasions. The first was Friday at dusk, and the second was midafternoon yesterday in the rain, and they were up to something serious."

"That's correct."

He smiled.

"You are a bright young man, Nate. I'm enjoying this very much."

He gestured toward the stuffed leather chair on the opposite side of the table from the rocker.

"Won't you sit down?"

I glanced at the chair.

"I'd love to, Mr. Barrow, but I really need to get back to my paper route."

I moved away from the fire another step.

"What were they doing that looked serious?"

"Please excuse me a minute, Nate—legs getting stiff."

He took a few guarded steps to the rocker, then turned and eased into the seat with the squeak of leather.

"Yes, of course, your paper route, very diligent of you. Let me see…serious. Well, as I said, the first time I saw the figures was last Friday evening."

His eyes brightened.

"I was on my widow's walk looking for Ollie, my pet gray owl, you see. Ollie's a big fellow with a six-foot wing span, and he usually glides by around dusk. He's not really a pet, you know, but I enjoy keeping up with him."

My eyebrows shot up. *The shadow!*

"That time, they were in the woods and headed toward the carriage house with a bundle, a heavy bundle apparently. They kept pausing as if to rest and to glance around as if they didn't want to be seen. Now mind you, it was almost dark; the woods are thick, and I could only get a glimpse here and there. And then, when they got close to the carriage house, I lost sight of them completely."

He rubbed his right knee.

"The second time, yesterday, when I saw them from my bedroom window, there were three of them. They had apparently come in from the driveway and looped around to the back of the carriage house where I lost them. I got a glimpse of them that time, but only a glimpse. I didn't see them leave."

"Can you describe them—the two the first time and the three the second?"

"I think so. I didn't recognize them, but I'd say the two I saw Friday were the same two I saw Saturday. Both were teenage boys, one very skinny, and both dressed like the hoodlums of today—jeans, black shoes, white T-shirts."

He shook his head.

"You know, Nate, today's teens have too much free time. All they do is watch TV or go to the movies and watch gangsters and hoodlums. It really saddens me."

His shoulders slumped.

"Really does."

"And the third one, sir, the third figure, the one you saw yesterday?"

"Ah, yes, the third one. Very peculiar. The third one was a teenage girl."

I dipped my head and raised my eyes and eyebrows to him.

"Teenage girl?"

"Yes, and in a dress. Very peculiar. In a dress and in the rain. I couldn't imagine why anyone planning to go into the woods would wear a dress, let alone in the rain."

*Uh-oh, Mammy.*

"Was it a…a black dress?"

"Yes, I believe it was."

I kind of stared at him a second while that news sank in, then I thanked him and excused myself with a promise to keep him updated on the case. He called for Wickers, who appeared out of nowhere and escorted me to the door. Mr. Barrow asked me to come back anytime.

I mounted my bike, then, on a hunch, I stopped at the carriage house and looked around for tire tracks. There were tire indentations in the weeds on the back side of the house, but the rain had washed away any tire tracks. Still, it was evidence enough for me.

I mounted up again, pedaled up the drive, then turned left. Tom Ray and his mother were in the next block down.

# CHAPTER 10
## FAT CHANCE

The Urdenbachs' house sat back from the others on the west side of Ridge Street and could have been there since the 1920s. At one time, it had probably been white with a narrow front porch. Now it was a moldy gray, and the porch only had room for a collection of rejected furniture: A sofa sprouting springs, a stuffed chair with bare wood showing through the arms, and even an old washing machine with rollers.

I had to walk by it on my way to school every morning, and over the last year, I'd learned the earlier I went by, the better. Tom Ray was not an early riser, but he was a good shot with his slingshot, and the chinaberry tree in his yard provided all the ammunition he needed. If we were late or he was early, we had to run and dodge our way through the hail of chinaberries.

Just in case he ever decided to get physical, Charlie would meet me at my house, leave his bike there, and we'd walk the fifteen minutes to school together. That hadn't happened yet, but today I was alone.

As I reached Ridge Street and turned left toward the school, I crossed my fingers and prayed Tom Ray was sleeping in on this Sunday and his mother would be answering the door.

At his house, a two-track driveway led to the back, where it stopped at a slumped one-car garage. In front of the garage sat an old coupe, like the '38 Plymouth Humphrey Bogart drove in *The Big Sleep,* but this one had a rusty roof and trunk. That old coupe plus the tall pines and bushes that lined the lot on both sides and the back—not to mention the overgrown front yard with the tall and scraggly chinaberry tree—gave the house a go-away feel.

I would have loved to have gone away, but I had to get paid for last week's papers. Mr. Glenn got his money upfront, so if I couldn't collect, the loss was mine, and I never would get that baseball glove I wanted. I turned right onto their cracked walkway, slid to a stop under the limbs of the chinaberry tree, then dismounted.

With their Sunday paper in hand, I jogged up the warped wooden steps. The only sound I heard was a barking dog from the lot behind their house. I knew from earlier collection attempts that the doorbell didn't work, so I stepped up to the rusty screen door, took a deep breath, and knocked.

I waited…nothing. No sounds, no signs of life.

I knocked again…still nothing.

I cocked my wrist to give it one more try when, from the

window to my right, the dingy white curtains parted. A woman wearing sunglasses with oversized oval lenses looked out at me. She had long, thin blonde hair like Mrs. Urdenbach, and she was short like Mrs. Urdenbach, but there weren't any lights on in the house, and she stayed behind the curtain and out of the daylight, so I couldn't be sure. I smiled at her and held up her paper. The curtains closed.

A few seconds later, the front door opened a crack, maybe three inches. I got a whiff of cigarette smoke, then a female voice said, "What do you want?"

"I have your Sunday paper, Mrs. Urdenbach, and I need to collect for last week's deliveries. I missed you on Friday."

A hand and a bruised wrist reached through the crack and unlatched the screen door.

"Give it to me."

I glanced down and took a breath.

"I'd love to, Mrs. Urdenbach, but I really need to collect for last week's papers first—it's the newspaper's policy now."

"Forty-five cents?"

"Yes, ma'am."

"I don't have it. Leave the paper, come back this Friday, and I'll pay for two weeks then."

"You know I can't do that, Mrs. Urdenbach. I have to collect today."

Inside I heard footsteps on their wooden floor.

"Who is it, Ma?"

The hand and wrist disappeared into the house.

"Paperboy."

The door creaked wide open, and the five-foot-ten, thirteen-year-old, career sixth-grader Tom Ray stepped into the light. From behind his long and stringy blond hair, his ice-blue eyes squinted at me.

"Leave the paper, Cowlick, and haul butt outta here."

"Tom Ray, it's only forty-five cents, but I've got to have it today. You know I've let you folks go before, but I can't do that anymore. It adds up. I'm in the hole."

He raised a pistol from behind his back.

"You're gonna be in a six-foot hole if you don't leave that paper and git."

I glanced at the gun, and it was real—definitely not a cap pistol. I sucked in a breath.

"I'll git, Tom Ray, but you'll have to do without your paper."

I turned for the steps.

The screen door squeaked, an explosion went off behind me, and splinters flew from the last board before the first step—the board my right foot was on. I took the next three steps and the six feet to my bike like a gazelle, but I didn't drop the paper.

Amid chips of chinaberry bark from another shot, I threw the paper into the basket, popped the kickstand into place, and spun that bike around in a blur.

*Man, that kid is crazy!*

I left that yard with a squealing rear tire and pedaled with my head down and legs pumping with strength I didn't know I had.

*Oh, Mammy, just get me past the trees on the edge of the lot!*

As I pedaled up the street and behind the trees, I heard Tom Ray laugh, but it was a forced laugh like he wanted me to hear it, but he really didn't think what had happened was that funny. You better believe I didn't think it was that funny—my knees shook all the way home.

When I reached my backyard and parked my bike, it occurred to me that the one-way shootout with Tom Ray wasn't funny for another reason: Now, I would need *two* new customers to get that baseball bat. But at least my Sunday deliveries were behind me, and I could try to relax and enjoy breakfast. I'd have to go to church, of course, but then the rest of the day would belong to Superman and me. Unless Mom insisted on those dancing lessons.

When I opened the gate to the Superman Suite, my knees and hands still shook. A nap was out of the question. I watered and exercised Superman, who stayed close by me as if he knew I needed comforting; then, as I didn't want to worry Mom, I went straight to Granddaddy. I found him in the kitchen between the stove and the refrigerator, laying out the eggs and bacon. I joined him at the counter.

"Where's Mom?"

He glanced over his shoulder.

"In her room getting dressed."

"Where's Becky?"

"I think she's still asleep on the sofa. Your mom threw her out of the bedroom last night—a major cat fight. I'm glad you slept through it. But I was proud of your mom. She went toe-to-toe with Becky and didn't back down."

He coughed into his bent arm.

"I tried to wake Becky a minute ago to see if she wanted breakfast, but she said, 'Buzz off.'"

I glanced toward the dining room. All clear.

"I got shot at this morning."

He stopped the egg in mid-crack, and egg white ran down the edge of the bowl.

"What?"

"Yes, sir. Tom Ray took two shots at me. Well, probably not directly at me, but close enough for me to get the message."

"Which was?"

"'We're not paying for our paper, and you can git.' So, I got."

"Two shots, huh. Okay, let's see now… You were shot at once yesterday by person or persons unknown, and you were shot at twice today by Tom Ray."

He tilted his head and looked at me with one eye half-closed.

"As Mammy would say, 'You might not be living on the right side of The Lord, young man.'"

I smiled.

"Well, it's Sunday, so maybe I can get back on the right side today."

I dropped the smile.

"But meanwhile, what do I do about Tom Ray? Do I report him to the police?"

"Hmm. Any witnesses?"

"I doubt it. Their house is pretty well screened off from the neighbors, plus it was seven-thirty on a Sunday morning, so...."

"How 'bout his mother, Libby? She's a nice lady, a loom operator at the mill. I've seen her at The Pig a few times with Fat Pat, the guy who helped me with the iron lung. He's kinda smitten with her and talks about her all the time."

He looked off into space. "But, he told me Friday that she was ill and didn't go in to work."

"She was there this morning, but she didn't look good, Granddaddy—bruised wrists. And wearing sunglasses. I thought that was strange."

"She's been dating that union guy—Alex somebody—and helping him organize some big rally coming up in a few weeks. Her husband left her about two years ago. Just took off. Maybe he's back and not happy about her dating. As I recall, he was abusive to her and Tom Ray, so maybe the glasses were to cover up a black eye."

"I guess so. Well, no witnesses, so forget it?"

"No, don't just forget it. Maybe it would be best to mention it to Detective Lewis but don't file any charges."

He cracked the last egg and poured it into the bowl.

"You know, sometimes bullies like Tom Ray have been bullied themselves, and now they're taking out their anger at the one who bullied them by being a bully to others."

He looked at me.

"Maybe killing him with kindness would work."

"Well, maybe. It hasn't worked with Becky."

He chuckled.

"No, I guess not. But that may be a special case."

He coughed into his arm again, then peeked around the refrigerator toward the dining room.

"Your mom knows you did the dishes yesterday, and Becky wasn't home; she found beggar's lice on Becky's socks in the dryer. We're going to powwow about her sometime today. Stay tuned."

Mom breezed into the kitchen in a yellow cotton dress, a white cardigan sweater, and her hair rolled up in a bun. She looked just like the old Mom, the relaxed Mom like she'd made a decision or come up with a plan she liked. She stepped over to me and gave me a big hug.

"How's our paperboy this beautiful morning?"

"Hungry for some breakfast with Sunday cinnamon rolls."

She opened the refrigerator door.

"Ah, you read my mind."

She took out a can of Pillsbury cinnamon rolls and pointed it at me.

"And this afternoon, how about some dancing lessons?"

"I think I'll just call in sick."

She grinned.

"Oh no you won't, you rascal; you'll be a dancing fool ready to rock and roll when I finish with you."

I moved out of her way.

"I'll be a fool all right—a fool with two left feet."

She cracked the cardboard can on the counter edge and twisted it open.

"Okay, 'Oh ye of little faith,' I'm going to let you in on a secret: Girls love to teach boys how to dance. If you learn the basics from me, they will delight in giving you remedial lessons at the party. Trust me."

Of course, I did trust her. After Sunday school and church, then a soup and sandwich lunch, I learned the classic six-count box step and a little one-two-three bop step. Mom assured me that would be enough to keep me from looking like the biggest square on the dance floor the next night, but I wasn't happy to learn both dances required holding hands.

Meanwhile, I had to bring Charlie and Chipper up to date on the case. I called Charlie and asked him to call Chipper.

We met at Chipper's house on North May Street, two blocks down and one block to the right.

Chipper's mom looked like Veronica Lake in *The Blue Dahlia*, a petite blonde with Veronica's long peek-a-boo hairstyle. And she always wore a smile too, like my mom. That is, like my mom when Becky was behaving. I figured Chipper must have gotten her Annette Funicello dark-brown hair and eyebrows from her dad. He was in the insurance business and always out, so I'd never met him. The best part was her mom loved dogs, so I knew she wouldn't mind if I brought Superman with me.

When Chipper and her mother came to the door, Superman beat whelps on my legs with his tail. Maybe he smelled the dog treats Chipper had in her hand. I don't know, but I smelled the chocolate chip cookies her mother brought with the lemonade.

We sat in the rockers on the wide front porch and talked about Donna's return from seeing her grandmother and Rose having her equestrian weekend washed out. Then, after her mother went back inside, we circled the rockers closer together, and I told them about the body, Mr. Barrow, the figures in the woods, and finally about Tom Ray. I didn't tell them about the girl in the black dress. That was family stuff, so I decided to keep that to myself.

Meanwhile, Superman stood at Chipper's feet and enjoyed

an occasional sit command followed by a dog treat and a scratch behind his ears.

Chipper leaned in.

"Wow, Tom Ray shot at you. Does that make him a suspect?"

"I don't know yet. It means he has the weapon that could have done it."

Charlie leaned in.

"That had to be Vinnie and Bones Mr. Barrow saw in his woods, so I think it's Vinnie. He's got a switchblade, so if he's got that, he's probably got a gun. Why else would he be trying to hide the body?"

I glanced at the front door.

"I don't know, but he could just be messing with us. I'm sure Becky told him about every move we've made."

Chipper leaned in again.

"Is Mr. Barrow out? I mean, you liked him, right?"

"I liked him, but he may have been nice just to throw me off. And he may have been lying about his gun being a pellet gun. Then there's Wickers, his butler. He's big enough to have carried that body into the woods all by himself."

I shook my head.

"But on the other hand, you don't kill someone and then leave the dead body on your property. I think Barrow's smarter than that."

Charlie wiped the crumbs of the last cookie off his lips, then leaned in again.

"Did Barrow have a black mustache? Did he smoke a cigar?"

"He had a gray mustache, and yes, he did smoke a cigar."

Charlie threw up his hands.

"Okay, then, that's our guy. We've seen enough westerns to know all the big-shot bad guys who control the outlaws have a black—or gray—mustache and smoke cigars."

I looked at him like *You can't be serious.*

"This is not a movie, Charlie."

"That doesn't mean he couldn't have ordered his man... What's his name?"

"Wickers."

"That doesn't mean he couldn't have ordered Wickers to eliminate the guy."

"But why? What's the motive? There has to be a motive."

Charlie glanced at the teakwood table with the empty cookie tray and reached for the last crumb.

"I don't know, but think about it, okay? Let's don't rule him out yet."

I looked at Chipper.

"Keep him in or rule him out?"

"In."

"Then he's in."

Charlie looked at his Lone Ranger watch, which had an image of the Lone Ranger and Tonto on its face, and stood.

"I gotta get home and rake some leaves before my allowance is threatened. I was supposed to do that yesterday, but...."

He pointed at me.

"Somebody had a better offer. Then it rained."

He dragged his rocker back to the wall.

"Nate, what say we go see Detective Lewis after school tomorrow and take him up on his offer of a Coke?"

I dragged mine to the wall and nodded.

"I like it."

We stepped off the porch and mounted up. Superman hesitated, then joined us. When we turned to wave goodbye, Chipper pointed at us.

"Don't forget the Halloween masks, and I'm counting on a dance with you guys. Don't make me a wallflower at my own party."

Charlie and I looked at each other, smiled, and read each other's minds: *Mary Elizabeth Chippenvale a wallflower? Fat chance of that.*

# CHAPTER 11
## THE CANDY CORN CLUE

The next morning, Charlie and I, with our baseball caps snug, collars turned up against the breeze, and books in hand, walked in front of Tom Ray's house at a pace like those Olympic walkers we'd seen in the theater newsreels. When we got past his chinaberry tree, we thought we were home free but then a chinaberry whistled by my head.

Tom Ray stepped out from behind a bush on the corner of the house, raised his slingshot, and fired another round.

I raised my books to the side of my head in time to block the shot, then we both took off in a run. One more chinaberry sailed by us before Tom Ray laughed.

"Don't be late for class, you creeps!"

It wasn't enough that we had to deal with that guy almost every morning; we had to deal with him in class, at lunch, and on the playground as well. And it wasn't like he was picking on just Charlie or me; he didn't like anybody. Lately, he had become such a nuisance in class that our teacher, Mrs. McAllister, or "Mrs. Mac," as we called her, had moved his desk to the front corner of the room so everyone could keep an eye on him. When he kept making faces at the kids on the front row and mouthing, *I'm gonna kill you,* Mrs. Mac moved his desk to the back corner by the coat rack and storage closet.

That's where his desk was that Monday morning, but as of 7:59, he hadn't shown up. He hadn't shown up last Friday either, so in one minute, he would be facing suspension.

It wasn't like Tom Ray was stupid. Okay, he was terrible at history, and to my knowledge, he had never passed a history test. But when he was in the mood, he was a math whiz and a great speller. The first spelling bee we had that year, he cleaned house, but after that, he would miss words on purpose so that he could sit down and read the comic book he always had in his back pocket.

And he had stolen math homework from other kids' lockers and copied it, but only because he didn't bother to write down the problems from the blackboard the day before. Sometimes he even corrected the homework before he stuffed it back into their locker. But he only did that for girls. I was just glad we might be without him that day.

When the bell rang, I looked over at Charlie in the row next to me and wiped my hand across my brow. He nodded.

At recess, Charlie and I went over to where a dump truck had left a steep pile of dirt near the corner of the playground. It looked like the principal had ordered it for some project and then changed his mind. That's where we played king of the hill. The rules were simple: No punching or kicking, and may the strong survive. Tom Ray ruled. Charlie and Monty Fryfogel, also known as "Big Fry," were the only kids in our grade who would challenge him. Sometimes a couple of seventh graders would try, but it usually took an eighth grader to get him off the hill.

That day Charlie and I decided we were a tag team like the ones I'd seen on Granddaddy's Sunday TV wrestling shows.

Charlie started by grabbing and shoving his way to the top of the pile, then stood his ground while Monty, Billy Westley, and the rest tried to throw him off. I waited until he was tired, and then I ran up, tagged him, and he left the fight to catch his breath.

I didn't last as long as Charlie, but at least I could handle Billy and a few others. Monty was another story. He wasn't that strong and couldn't see well without his glasses, but he was tall, heavy, and hard to move. After a struggle, he gave me a final push. His leg just happened to be in my way, so I tripped over it and tumbled off the hill.

At the bottom, Charlie helped me up, handed my windbreaker to me, then we decided to go over to the swings and watch the girls. On a windy day, their dresses would fly up. They acted embarrassed, but sometimes I wondered if they let it happen on purpose, especially Candy Crocker. She was eleven going on eighteen.

From behind us, Monty yelled, "I'm the king of the hill!"

We looked back, and he stood on top of the hill with his arms raised. At the bottom, five sixth-grade boys stood with their hands on their hips and their chests heaving.

I looked at Charlie and grinned.

"Wanna go back and dethrone that tyrant?"

He laughed.

"Nah, let him enjoy his day. We'll get him tomorrow."

All six swings were occupied when we got there. Chipper, Rose, and Donna were on one side, and Molly Fryfogel, Monty's petite little twin, known as "Little Fry," Candy, and Beth Kline, another blonde like Molly and Rose, were on the other. When we strolled past, all six girls giggled about something. Of course, we didn't stop or comment because that would look like we were interested. I made a note to ask them what was so funny at the party. I suspected it had something to do with the mud caked on our tennis shoes and the knees of our jeans.

When we passed Candy, she flew her swing really high, flashed her panties at us, and winked at Charlie. At least it looked like she winked at Charlie. She'd been flirting with him since Chipper sent invitations to the party weeks earlier. I looked at Charlie, but if he noticed, he didn't show it.

When we got to the water fountain against the school's brick wall, I watched him drink up.

"Can you dance, Charlie?"

He stood straight and wiped his mouth with the back of his hand.

"Of course, I can dance."

I grinned.

"I don't mean the 'Hi—ya—ya—ya—Hi—ya—ya—ya' kind of dance."

I bent over to take a drink, and as soon as the water arched up, he pushed my face into it.

He laughed.

"Now you, Chief Rain in Face. Maybe that rain dance you do, huh?"

With eyes closed, I wiped my face with my hands, then pulled my shirttail out of my pants to dry it.

"Wow, me must have big medicine. One little 'Hi—ya' and it rains."

He threw his arm around my shoulder and gave me a rough hug.

"Yeah, you have big medicine all right. I saw the way Candy winked at you back there."

I pulled my shirt down and opened my eyes.

"Winked at me? No no, Charlie, she winked at you."

Charlie furrowed his brow.

"Me?"

"Yes, you, you stud. Just wait. Tonight, she's going to be on you like trail dust on drovers."

He shook his head.

"Better not be."

After school, we sprinted past Tom Ray's house, then

quick-marched up my street. On our way past Tom Ray's, I noticed another car in his driveway, a late model, medium blue Ford. I'd seen it before but didn't know who owned it. Charlie didn't know either.

At home, I watered and exercised Superman. Then, from the kitchen, I called the SPPD while Charlie consumed a few Ritz crackers with peanut butter. From Mom and Becky's bedroom, the Penguins sang "Earth Angel."

Mom answered. She said Detective Lewis would see us right away, then she said, "Is Becky home?"

"I just got home, Mom, but I hear the radio."

"Look for her, please."

"Ah…yes, ma'am."

I put down the phone, walked to the bedroom door, and knocked.

No answer.

I knocked again. Still no answer.

I tried the door, but it was locked. That meant she'd gone out the window. I'd overheard Mom tell her that morning she was to come straight home from school, so she must have come in just long enough to make it look like she was home and then bailed.

I walked back to the phone but looked around the house on the way—no Becky. Then I had a hunch and jogged back to the living room. Through the window, I saw her at the streetlight beside Vinnie.

Mr. Cool wore his black hair slicked back in a duck's tail, the collar of his black leather jacket turned up, and his black leather motorcycle boots inside the legs of his jeans. He held a cigarette in one hand and Becky in the other.

*Crap.* I trudged back to the phone.

"She's not in the house, Mom. She's outside."

She let out a long sigh.

"Where outside, Nate? And don't lie to me."

*Double crap.*

"She's ah… She's at the streetlight with Vinnie."

She took a breath.

"Okay, thanks. Dan will be here all afternoon, so come on down."

I hung up and turned to Charlie.

"Detective Lewis is there, and he's waiting on us. Let me get my paper sack with the suspicious leaf, and we'll roll."

I stepped for my room, then stopped and turned.

"Hey, you still have that piece of candy corn you found, right? You brought it with you, right?"

He wiped cracker crumbs from his mouth.

"Ah…well, actually I forgot it. I guess it's still in my jeans."

"Still in your jeans? Valuable evidence still in your jeans? Come on, Charlie!"

"Yeah, I guess, but it's okay; I don't think Mom has done the wash yet. Want me to go home and get it?"

I shook my head.

"No…too late now; we need to get down there."

I walked toward my room.

"I'll get my evidence bag and meet you out back."

"Okay, I'll be entertaining my buddy Superman. He likes me more than you anyhow!"

"Ha!"

A few minutes later, we rolled up in front of the Southern Pines Police Department on Broad Street and popped our bikes into the bike rack on the sidewalk.

The SPPD headquarters, a white cinder block building, stood behind a huge magnolia tree with a sidewalk that led under the tree's limbs to the front door. We walked along that sidewalk and entered.

Inside the building, we stood in a twenty-by-twenty main office divided across the middle by an oak counter. The counter had one of those raise-up panels on the right that allowed access to the back. A fluorescent light in the ceiling above the counter lit the room.

Behind the counter, Mom sat at her desk on the right with her head down and a pencil in her hand. A desk for the duty officer, occupied by Officer Lum at the time, sat next to Mom to her right with a black trash can between them. Last year's rubber plant sat in a big clay pot on the floor in the corner to my left. Chief McDonald's office took up the far-right corner, Detective Lewis's office was next to the chief, and there were two jail cells behind a door on the left side.

Four heavy wooden chairs sat against the wall facing the counter, and a Coke vending machine and trash can stood against the wall to my right. Charlie and I stepped up to the counter and elbowed each other when we saw a box of donuts on Mom's desk.

Mom looked up over the baby rubber plant on her desk and smiled.

"Hi, boys. Dan will be with you in a minute."

She put her pencil down and stood, then stepped around the desk and moved the box of donuts to the counter. She plopped two nickels on the counter beside it and winked.

"From Dan, and help yourself to the donuts."

Officer Lum, a Korean American and Army veteran, sat with a black phone held to his ear and his blue tie loose under the collar of his blue shirt. As we picked up the nickels, he waved, then looked down and made notes on the yellow pad on his desk. In front of the pad, a cigarette streamed smoke from a half-full ashtray.

I smiled and waved back, but I doubted if he saw me.

Meanwhile, the air conditioner in the window behind me on the left hummed along and pumped in fresh air. Despite the air conditioner and Mom's plants, the place still smelled stale and moldy, like sweaty laundry that had been left in a smoke-filled room too long.

Charlie stuck his nickel in the slot, pressed down on the lever, then the six-ounce Coke clattered into the exit slot in the center of the machine. He pried off the cap with the opener, and the cap clattered into the bin inside. I followed with my nickel.

Charlie had his first bite of donut in his mouth, and my Coke had just banged into the slot when Detective Lewis, in a white shirt and red paisley tie, opened his door. He smiled and waved.

"Come in, boys."

We entered with a donut in one hand and a Coke in the other. With eyes wide, I checked out the first detective's office I'd ever seen in person. It was definitely not Sergeant Friday's office but just big enough for a standard-size oak desk, three five-foot-tall filing cabinets on the left wall, a coat rack next to the cabinets, a trash can by the desk, and two oak chairs in front of the desk. Tan cinder block walls. The desk faced the door, and venetian blinds were in the window. No curtains.

Mom had mentioned the absence of curtains to me before and had been working on Lewis to correct that oversight.

A photo of President Eisenhower and another of the American flag hung from the wall on our right. A framed military document hung between the president and the flag, probably Lewis's honorable discharge.

We sat in the chairs. Lewis sat at his desk. Mom appeared with a smile and handed us a paper towel each. I stuffed the last quarter of the donut into my mouth, licked my fingers, then took the towel from her and said a garbled, "Thanks, Mom."

She frowned at me. *Oops.* You're not supposed to talk with food in your mouth.

As she closed the door behind her, Lewis took a yellow legal pad from his desk drawer. He reached for a pencil in the clay beer mug on the corner of his desk. A black phone sat in the other corner. No ashtray, which explained why I found it easier to breathe in that room.

"Okay, boys, here's the situation: We have the search warrant, but the chief still says hold off until we have more proof that we'll find something. I still have the fountain pen you found at the scene, and that could fit into the puzzle later, but I need more. Do you have anything else for me that could make a case for exercising the warrant now?"

Charlie looked at me, which I took to mean I was to go first, so I cleared my throat and held out my evidence bag to him.

"Inside this bag is a leaf I took from the crime scene. If you have it analyzed, I believe you'll find a blood spot against a vein in the leaf."

He took the bag, made a note on top of it, then pulled the leaf out and examined it.

"Oh, yeah, that black spot is blood, I'm sure of it."

He looked up.

"I'll send it to Raleigh, and if they confirm it's blood, we'll get that search warrant."

"Thank you, sir. Now, there's more."

I told him about looking for the body on Sunday morning, my visit with Mr. Barrow, the two teenagers, and the tire indentations in the weeds by the driveway. I didn't mention the third teenager.

"Okay, we're back to no corpse, but at least we have a witness that confirms something suspicious was going on in the woods on Friday evening and Saturday afternoon."

He made a note on his pad, then looked up.

"And Mr. Barrow says his rifle is a pellet gun, and you say his butler is big enough to have moved the body by himself?"

"Yes, sir. And don't forget the tire indentations. A car was there after we found the body."

He made another note.

"Anything else?"

I glanced at Charlie as if looking for his okay for what I was about to say next. He nodded.

"Then I was shot at on Sunday morning."

"Again? On the Barrow property?"

"No, sir. The shots came from Tom Ray Urdenbach after they refused to pay for their paper, and I refused to give them the Sunday paper."

He pursed his lips and shook his head.

"But I don't think he was trying to hit me. He was in the

doorway, and I was leaving his porch when the first shot hit the porch floor, then the second hit the chinaberry tree next to where I was mounting my bike."

He reached into the right-hand drawer of his desk and pulled out a form, so I leaned forward.

"But there weren't any witnesses, so I don't want to file charges."

He plopped the form on top of his legal pad.

"I won't file this if you don't want me to, but I think I should at least get your charges on record. It's not the first time young Urdenbach has been the subject of a complaint."

I set my Coke on the floor and put my hands on the edge of his desk.

"But I don't think there is any connection to the case. Well, other than the fact that Tom Ray has a weapon that could have killed the guy."

He said as he wrote, "Maybe a connection, maybe not."

As Lewis continued writing, Charlie looked at me and slid his hand with extended fingers across his throat. I nodded, then shrugged and slid back into my chair.

Lewis set his pencil down on the desktop, tossed the form into a wire basket in the center of his desk, and looked up.

"Okay, boys, back to those two teenagers in the woods."

He picked up his pencil and tapped it on the yellow pad.

"You said Mr. Barrow described them as one skinny, both in jeans, black shoes, white T-shirts."

"Yes, sir."

"Can you identify them?"

I glanced at Charlie and then back to Lewis.

"You mean like in a lineup?"

He smiled.

"No, Nate. No lineup. I was just asking if you can think of two teens who match that description."

"Well, I guess I could think of several I've seen in the high school part of our school, but the two I think of first are Vinnie Marcello and Bones Meacham."

He made notes.

"Bones?"

"Yes, sir. I don't know his first name. He's so skinny and boney everyone has called him Bones as long as we've lived here."

Lewis looked up.

"Charlie?"

Charlie shrugged.

"Beats me, sir. That's all I've ever heard him called."

"Charlie, would those two be the ones that come to mind for you, or can you think of someone else?"

"Those are the only two. But Vinnie lives next door to Mr. Barrow, so that might be important."

Lewis wrote that down.

"Yes, could be."

Then he tapped his pencil on the pad again.

"Nate, did Mr. Barrow give you any other description of those teenagers in his woods? Height? Hair color?"

*Well, yes, but...* "No, sir. But Vinnie has a new car, a '55 Chevy. Those tire indentations could have come from his car."

He made another note.

"Okay, back to Mr. Barrow. Did he describe any sounds or smells?"

"No, sir. He's pretty hard of hearing, but he talked with his butler, Wickers, Saturday night after you'd called, and Wickers told him he thought he'd heard a shot Friday afternoon and another Saturday morning. Actually, he was certain of the one Saturday morning."

"Okay."

He wrote something else and then put his pencil down.

"Anything else?"

Charlie and I looked at each other, then back to Lewis, and shook our heads.

"Okay, boys, I guess that's it for now."

He stood.

"I'll let you know if we need to talk again. Meanwhile, Nate..."

I picked up my Coke from the floor and stood.

"Yes, sir."

"Don't go near the Urdenbachs."

"Yes, sir. We have to pass his house on our way to school,

but that's as close as I'll get. And thank you for the Cokes and donuts."

He smiled.

"My pleasure."

He looked at Charlie.

"And you boys come again. I still want to hear more about your family, Charlie."

"Yes, sir. After we help you solve this case, we'll be back."

On our way out, I asked Mom if we could have another donut. She nodded, so we drained our Cokes, dropped the empty bottles in the wooden Coke crate on the floor by the machine, then grabbed a donut and hustled out the door.

Outside in the bright sun and cool breeze, Charlie and I window-shopped the sporting goods in the window of the hardware store down from the police station. They had the Wilson infielder's glove I wanted. We finished off our donuts, licked our fingers, wiped our hands on our jeans, then returned to our bikes in the bike rack and mounted up.

As we pedaled up Orchard Road, Charlie had that wrinkled brow look like he was deep in thought. He was probably trying to figure out how he would dodge Miss Crocker at the party.

"Okay, Charlie, what's on your mind?"

"Oh, nothing."

"Candy Crocker, maybe?"

"No, definitely not her."

He looked at me.

"Nate, did you notice what was on the far end of the counter at the police office?"

"You mean the rubber tree plant?"

"No, on the counter, a bowl of candy corn. It was on top of some corn husks like they had it displayed for Halloween."

"Wow. I wonder if my mom did that. If so, she could tell me when she did it and who's been into it."

I shook my head.

"I guess we should have asked her about it. Candy corn seems to be popping up all over this case."

"Sure does, but don't worry; I'll find that piece of corn as soon as I get home, and we'll get it to Detective Lewis later."

We pedaled along in silence for a minute, and then I looked over at him.

"How 'bout those masks? Do you need any help with them?"

He smiled.

"Nope. They're ready to go."

"Well, will you tell me who we're supposed to be tonight?"

"Nope."

"Then just tell me you're not Prince Charming, and I'm not Cinderella."

He threw his head back.

"Ha! That's not a bad idea."

He looked over at me.

"But no, nobody will confuse us with Prince Charming and Cinderella."

"Okay. I'm counting on it."

We had come to the Ridge Street intersection, so we both stood on our pedals and picked up the pace.

# CHAPTER 12
## A BUMP IN THE LAKE

Charlie's parents were friends with the Chippenvales, so they wanted to get to the party early and help with the decorations. Charlie and I didn't want to go early; we had other plans. I mean, the party was great, but Halloween night was our one chance a year to stock up on candy, so as far as we were concerned the party could wait. Mom agreed to take us later, so after supper Charlie's parents dropped him off at our house and we hit the street.

We weren't in the rich area of town like Charlie, but we'd learned that the rich weren't always the most generous, plus their houses were usually spaced farther apart. In my neighborhood, we could cover more houses in less time. Just to test the generosity theory and over Charlie's protests, we started with Mr. Barrow.

Charlie had brought our party masks in a paper sack and wouldn't let me see them, so we left them at the house and wore our Halloween masks from the year before; I was Frankenstein, and he was a werewolf, which seemed appropriate with a bright half-moon lighting our way down Barrow's driveway.

The long, dark porch awaited us, but when we stepped up to the front door, I could tell through the leaded glass a light was on in the house. I pulled the handle beside the door and heard a bell clang in the interior.

We waited. Then Charlie, the werewolf, looked at me.

"Not home. Let's go."

I held up my hand.

The light in the ceiling of the porch came on. The door creaked, then opened. Wickers, in his penguin costume, stepped into the light and loomed over us.

We looked up. I held out my grocery sack.

"Trick-or-treat!"

If a stone could smile then, Wickers smiled.

"I see. Goblins. Wait here, children, I won't be a moment."

A minute later, I heard footsteps and a *tap, tap, tap* on the marble floor. Mr. Barrow appeared with Wickers behind him looking over his shoulder. Barrow leaned on his cane and smiled.

"Well, good evening, Sir Goblins."

He glanced back at Wickers.

"We certainly don't want any tricks played on us tonight, do we, Wickers?"

"Certainly not, sir."

"Then what have we to treat these scary goblins so as to avoid that calamity?"

Wickers handed him the treats. Mr. Barrow extended two large Hershey bars, then dropped one at a time into each of our empty sacks. They hit bottom with a paper snap.

Charlie and I looked at each other.

*A whole large Hershey bar!*

Mr. Barrow cocked his head and smiled.

"I do enjoy my Hershey bars. I buy them by the case and I'm happy to share them with you."

He put his hand to his chin.

"That wouldn't happen to be Master Nathan Hawke behind that Frankenstein mask, would it?"

I lifted the mask over my head.

"Yes, sir, Mr. Barrow. Good evening."

I held out my hand to Charlie.

"And this is my friend Charles Shonkasabe."

Charlie took his mask off and nodded.

"Good to meet you, Charles. And thank you both for coming by. We haven't had trick-or-treaters in years, maybe twenty years."

He stepped back as if to retire, then stopped.

"Oh, Nate?"

"Yes, sir?"

He looked at Charlie and then back to me.

"Can we talk?"

I glanced at Charlie.

"Oh, yes, sir. Charlie knows about the case. He's been with me."

"Well then, what's the latest?"

"In a nutshell, no body, no case, no police investigation."

"Any newspaper involvement? I didn't see anything in your paper this morning."

"Not that I know of. Chief McDonald seems to be keeping this very quiet."

"Well, I don't doubt that you saw a body, and I don't doubt I saw the people who removed the body so that body will turn up eventually. When it does, I want this thing closed as quickly and quietly as possible."

He cleared his throat and pulled the maroon robe closer to his body.

"To that end, you and your friend Charles may do any investigations you need to do in my woods. *But*, I don't want any more police cars, policemen, or detectives on my property. I don't want to take a chance of some news photographer taking a photograph of that. Agreed?"

Charlie and I said in unison, "Yes, sir."

"Thank you."

He reached for the door.

"Now, please excuse me. I've got to get out of this cool air."

We waved goodbye with a chorus of "Good night."

The rest of our brief trick-or-treating went without incident. Our candy stores were replenished with Milk Duds, suckers, Lemon Drops, and little bags of candy corn, the most popular.

At eight o'clock, with Becky sulking in her bedroom and Granddaddy handing out candy to trick-or-treaters, we rolled out of our driveway for the ten-minute drive to Aberdeen Lake and my dancing debut.

On the way, with Mom driving and Charlie and me in the back seat, Charlie pulled out our masks and handed one to me. They were full-face masks with cut-outs for eyes and mouth and a horseshoe-shaped flap for the nose. Both were made from heavy grocery sack paper and had rubber bands linked together for a strap.

Charlie, the artist, had painted the front side of his mask in war paint. On a light tan background, a black handprint covered his mouth area with fingers extended up his right cheek and the thumb up the left like he'd dipped his left hand in a puddle of black paint, then pressed his hand against the mouth and cheeks of the mask. Across the top of the forehead, he'd painted a wide white band with a zigzag red line to make a headband. A reddish-tan color highlighted the eyes and temples. He slipped it on.

"What do you think? I'm Black Dog, Osage warrior."

"I think you look more like Chief Shut-my-mouth."

He pushed me against my door.

"What? Maybe I'll shut your mouth!"

I smiled.

"Just kidding, Black Dog. It looks good, very good. Very authentic."

I looked up to see Mom smile at us in the rearview mirror.

My mask featured a white forehead and a black Lone Ranger mask around the eyes and over the temples. A red line highlighted the top edge of the Lone Ranger mask and a white line highlighted the bottom. From the bottom white line, blue lines streamed from below the eyes on both sides down to the jawline. I slipped it on.

"Okay, Black Dog, who am I?"

"You 'Kemosabe Rain in Face.'"

"'Kemosabe Rain in Face?' You just had to get in another shot, didn't you?"

"Yep. You had it coming."

I slipped it off and examined it again.

"Well, I like it. You really are an artist, Charlie. No joke."

As Mom pulled into the gravel parking lot at the lake, Candy Crocker stepped out of a blue Ford sedan that had stopped perpendicular to the parking spaces. She wore a plain brown eye mask and a single-feather headdress.

I smiled, elbowed Charlie, and pointed at her. He elbowed me back with a little more oomph and shot me a scorching frown. Mom parked against a railroad tie and we hopped out with our masks in place.

Between the parking lot and the lake lay a concrete slab.

From a record player on a table on that slab, Chuck Berry sang, "Maybellene, why can't you be true..." Strings of small white lights strung from poles on the corners of the slab lighted the tables and chairs along the edges where the Chippenvales and Shonkasabes sat.

Like boxers in their separate corners, the kids stood in two groups, one for girls and one for boys. Charlie and I stopped at Mom's window to thank her and say goodbye, and then Charlie strolled toward the party. Mom reached out and patted my arm.

"Get in there and boogie-woogie, Nate. Spread yourself around, be good to the girls, and have fun."

"Yes, ma'am."

As a yellow car I recognized as the Fryfogels' Buick rolled into the parking lot, I jogged away and caught up with Black Dog.

Even with their masks on, it wasn't hard to tell who was who. On the girls' side, Candy Crocker was Tiger Lily from *Peter Pan*; Rose was some kind of Arabian princess, maybe Jasmine; Donna—the tallest girl—was Wonder Woman, and Chipper was Cinderella. She was still the cutest. As long as I had to dance with somebody, I hoped it would be her.

Chipper, and all the other girls, wore sweaters with collars and swing skirts with fluffy layers underneath.

On our side, Billy Westley, a redhead with freckles and a gap in his front teeth, made it easy by wearing a Howdy Doody mask. While the rest of us wore sweaters or jackets and slacks, Billy went full Howdy with a red cowboy bandanna around his neck, a denim jacket, and jeans for pants. He stood with a boy I didn't recognize.

When Charlie and I joined them, Billy introduced the stranger as Bobby Olsen, Rose's boyfriend from a private school in Raleigh. Bobby had a blond crewcut, wore a wolf facemask, and looked to be a seventh or eighth grader, maybe two inches taller than me and an inch taller than Charlie. He was quick to offer his hand, and his voice was pleasant enough, but it had a superior tone.

Monty Fryfogel joined us, and Molly, or "Little Fry," joined the girls. Molly wore a yellow mask sprinkled with gold flakes and had her blonde hair done in a ponytail. Big Fry wore a green mask with a matching green peaked hat like he was either Robin Hood or Peter Pan. He pointed at Molly.

"Sorry, guys. Molly insisted on being Tinker Bell, and I had to be Peter Pan."

He shook his head.

"You know Peter Pan was really a woman, right? Mary Martin to be exact."

Billy gave him a light shove.

"No, he wasn't."

Big Fry, the most well-read student in our class, shrugged.

"I'm sorry to burst your bubble, Howdy Doody, but although the author of *Peter Pan*, Sir James Barrie, wrote Peter

Pan as a boy who could fly, the part of Peter Pan on the stage has been played by a woman since 1904."

Billy made a fist and his neck turned red.

"Peter Pan was no woman, Monty! Take that back!"

Just as Billy was about to do something really stupid that would anger the normally calm Big Fry and leave Billy with a bad case of empty holster, the music stopped. Everyone turned to the Chippenvales.

Mrs. Chippenvale, the blonde Veronica Lake look-alike, took her hand off the portable record player and smiled up at the six-foot, dark-skinned, and slightly heavy gentleman with her. Behind them, the Shonkasabes removed the table-cloth that covered the items on the table and exposed food and drinks.

The gentleman wore a tweed sports coat and plaid tie, and I assumed he was Chipper's dad because he had the same complexion and dark curly hair as her. He stepped into the center of the concrete slab and held up his hands.

"Kids, Mrs. Chippenvale and I and Mary Elizabeth would like to thank all of you for coming. And thank you for wearing your masks—very creative."

He smiled and rubbed his hands together.

"Now, we've got a couple of games planned for you and then a little dancing, but first...."

He pointed at the table.

"You may remove your masks and help yourself to the drinks and snacks. Happy Halloween!"

After Black Dog and I had finished our Dr Peppers, a muffin, and a few chocolate chip cookies, I looked around. Most of the girls had hurried back to their corner. The exception was Candy "Tiger Lily" Crocker, who continued to hang around us and may have read too much into the fact that she and Charlie were both disguised as Indians.

A few minutes later, Mr. Chippenvale stepped forward again and announced that the first game would be a corn toss. He divided us into two teams of three boys and three girls, and the objective was to toss more little bags of candy corn into our bowl than the other guys got in their bowl.

When he announced the teams, I looked at Charlie.

"Lucky you, Black Dog, Tiger Lily is with us."

He shot me a look.

"Knock it off."

I had noticed two canoes, each with two paddles, pulled up on the sand on the right side of the fishing pier. They had the look of game number two, but first we had to play the corn toss game. That was fine with me; I just wanted to run out the clock.

I threw last for the red team, but it was Tiger Lily going three for three ahead of me that beat the blues by two bags. Team Captain Charlie, with Tiger Lily beside him (a little too close beside him based on the creases in Charlie's forehead), selected one of the two wrapped prizes. The prize turned out to be six 45 RPM records that included recordings by Little Richard, Chuck Berry, and The Platters.

Blond Bobby of the Raleigh private school looked into our box.

"Ah. I've already got all of those."

We divided the records based on who already had what. I didn't have any of them, so I took the last one, which turned out to be "Sh-Boom," my favorite.

Then Chipper's dad stepped forward again, this time wearing rubber boots. He smiled.

"Is there anyone here who can't swim?"

No one raised their hand, so he nodded, "Okay."

He pointed at the canoes. "Well, there are life preservers in each canoe, plus I will be on the pier with a rescue buoy if needed. We have cleaned these canoes thoroughly, but I know some of you girls may not want to risk your good clothes."

He turned and looked at Mr. Shonkasabe, who pointed at him with a knowing smile.

"And, truth be known, I may not have thought this one through very well."

He shrugged.

"Therefore, if any of you had rather not participate in the next game, which is a tag-team canoe race around the pier, just let me know, and we'll adjust the teams."

No one begged off, so we followed Mr. Chippenvale down

to the pier and canoes, dimly lit by the lights from the dance area.

He stopped by the first canoe and raised his hand to silence the girls' henhouse chatter.

"We'll keep the same teams, but we want you to pair up boy-girl for the race. When I say go, the first two from each team will launch their canoe and race around the pier and back to the beach on the other side of the pier. Then the next two on your team will change places with the first two and race back to this side. Then the final two. Now, we don't want anyone getting their shoes wet, so Mr. Shonkasabe and I…."

He pointed to his feet.

"In our rubber waders will assist every launch and every landing. Team captains, organize your teams and stand by your canoe when ready."

Charlie and I grabbed the canoe closest to the pier—the inside track—then Charlie decided I would go first and he would be the anchor man. Tiger Lily would be with me, a strategic decision by Charlie that had nothing to do with winning, and Chipper would be with Charlie.

The blue team went with Molly, wearing her Tinker Bell mask again, and Monty, now wearing his horn-rimmed glasses, paddling first, and Rose with Bobby the anchors.

It wasn't until I got in the back of the canoe, gripped the paddle, and awaited the go signal that I realized I'd never paddled a canoe. I'd seen it done in movies and on TV shows, of course, but never actually done it. I said a quick prayer that I could fake it long enough to get us to the other side of the pier right side up.

"Go!"

Mr. Shonkasabe gave us a shove that rocked Candy backward and pulled her paddle out of the water, so it was all me on the first stroke. Which wasn't enough. At the same time, Mr. Chippenvale launched Monty and Molly, who had apparently been to summer camp a few times and knew what they were doing. They paddled off, leaving a wake of foamy water behind them.

Candy, with her single-feather headdress now flopped over one eye, got her paddle back in the water and we fell in behind Monty and Molly at their pace but definitely not gaining on them. Meanwhile, back on the beach, the screams from the fans could have been heard in Aberdeen.

As Monty approached the end of the twenty-yard-long pier, the masked Molly, paddling on the right side, accidentally splashed water on her dress. She stopped paddling to brush it off just as Monty made a strong pull on the left side and they sailed off into the night.

I saw an opportunity, but just as we got to the end of the pier and into the turn, we bumped into something in the water and jerked to a wobbly stop.

Candy leaned over the bow, then dropped her paddle,

slapped her hands to her headband, and let out a blood-curdling scream that froze the crowd and gave me goosebumps.

I leaned forward.

"What? What?"

She turned, sobbing, hands covering her eyes.

"Back up! Back up!"

I back-paddled and felt the canoe slip off whatever we'd hit.

"What, what's wrong?"

"Oh, God, Nate! A dead man! It rolled over and looked right at me!"

"Well, look the other way, quick!"

I reversed stroke, paddled forward, and there it was, bobbing in the water in a fetal position—blue tie, dirty white shirt, Hollywood blond hair...our itinerant corpse.

Thirty minutes later, after Mr. Chippenvale had driven to the police station to get help and call the other parents, Detective Lewis arrived in the white Nash patrol car with the bubble gum machine flashing bright red and the siren wailing.

The party ended, and my dancing debut was put on hold.

# CHAPTER 13
## THE DEAD GUY

After the Shonkasabes brought me home in their Chrysler station wagon, Mom called me into the kitchen. I entered and got a whiff of fresh coffee. She and Granddaddy sat at the kitchen table with coffee cups before them. No smiles and no music from Mom and Becky's bedroom. I wanted to tell them about the body, but I sensed that was not the time.

I stopped beside Mom at the end of the table, and she took my hand.

"Get some milk or water and sit with us a minute, Nate. I know it's late and a school night, but we've got something we need to discuss with you."

"It's okay, Mom. I'm not thirsty."

I sat in the chair against the wall.

"What's up?"

She sighed.

"Becky's not home. We assume she's with Vinnie. Have you seen her?"

"No, ma'am. Not since we left for the party."

She looked at the table and rubbed her temples with her fingertips.

"Well, we had a talk with her this evening. A difficult talk."

Granddaddy cleared his throat.

"More like one of Mammy's 'come to Jesus' moments."

Mom held up her hand to Granddaddy and looked at me.

"I called a friend of your father's today—Jess Wilkerson. He's the chief financial officer of a Catholic boarding school in Charlotte. Your father was Catholic, and he and Jess were in Catholic school and the Marines together. We knew Jess and his wife, Janice, at Cherry Point. I don't think we've told you this before, but because your father wanted it that way, Becky was baptized a Catholic, and so were you."

She picked up her coffee cup but realized it was empty and put it back in the saucer.

"Because she was baptized a Catholic, Jess thinks he can get her a scholarship to his school."

I leaned forward.

"She's going to a boarding school?"

She shook her head.

"That hadn't been decided when we talked with her. We just explained that boarding school was an option for us. In other words, shape up, or we'll ship you out."

She choked up on the words "ship you out" and reached for the napkin by the saucer.

She dabbed her eyes with the napkin and blew out a breath.

"That was the gist of it, but I actually said, 'If you choose to disobey me or your granddaddy one more time, we may choose to exercise that option.' I explained that for the time being, she could choose her school and her friends, but if she continued to listen to them and not to us, she would forfeit her right to choose, and we would make that school location decision for her."

She pointed her finger at me.

"And that would go for you too, Nate. If at any time you start choosing your friends over us and making bad decisions, we could find a school for you too."

*Wow.* I sat back in my seat and thought of Bobby Olsen. I didn't want to go to school with jerks like him. *No thank you.*

Granddaddy coughed into his bent arm and cleared his throat.

"And now she's gone again, Nate, and apparently out the bedroom window while we were in the living room. And she took clothes and cosmetics with her. So, it's your mother's decision, but as far as I'm concerned, she's burned her last bridge."

I put my hands on the table.

"Want me to go look for her? I could start at Vinnie's house. Have you called Vinnie or his mom?"

"Yes, I have, but his mom sounded...well, she wasn't very coherent. I think she said Vinnie wasn't home and she hadn't seen Becky."

"Well, that's a big house; they could be there. Let me go look. If Vinnie's car is there, she may be there."

"No, Nate. I'll call Dan. I think the situation could be described as a runaway teen now, so he would be the one to do the investigation."

She checked the clock on the wall.

"It's nine-fifty. If she's not home by ten, I'll call him."

"Please, Mom. Let me go look first."

I stood.

"I could be there and back before ten. I mean, they could be in the swing on the back porch or just sitting in his car."

Mom looked at Granddaddy. He nodded.

Five minutes later, I jogged down the Marcello's concrete driveway toward the double garage at the end. It was separate from the two-story, white brick house on my right. As I took the sidewalk to the garage's side door, headlights lit the yard on the other side of the driveway, and a car turned onto the drive. I slipped behind the holly bush next to the side door.

Vinnie's red and white Chevy, now with the top up, stopped in front of the white garage door. The headlights reflecting off the door revealed Vinnie in the driver's seat wearing his hoodlum outfit and Becky in the passenger seat in a white blouse and pink sweater—the only passenger.

Vinnie cut the lights and engine, said something to Becky, then got out and marched toward the back porch.

I waited until he was in the house, and then I stepped out

from behind the bush and jogged over to Becky's side of the car.

She saw me coming and rolled down her window.

"Get outta here, Nate!"

I put my hands on the windowsill.

"What are you doing, Becky? Mom and Granddaddy are worried sick. I left Mom in tears."

"Well, they oughta be worried sick, damn it! They're sending me away."

"No, they aren't! At least not yet. That's just an option if you keep doing stupid stuff like this."

"It's too late. I'm leaving. *We're* leaving."

"We?"

"Yes, we. I love him and he loves me, and we're getting out of this crummy town."

"Ah, come on, Becky, think about it. No education, no money, no job. Just give yourself and Mom another chance. She loves you; I love you; we can work this out."

"Vinnie's got plenty of money, and education is stinkin' BS! We'll be fine."

"Becky! Come on, give us another chance."

"No!"

She put her face in her hands and sobbed.

"It's too late; we've got to go."

"Hey, punk! Get away from my car!"

I turned. Vinnie stepped off the porch and approached me

with a suitcase in one hand and a crude-looking pistol in the other.

I held up my hands.

"Get over there where I can see you."

He pointed the pistol at a large oak tree on the other side of the driveway.

Without taking my eyes off him, I walked around the front of the car, then stopped at the tree trunk.

Meanwhile, he followed me around the car and stopped at the driver's side.

Becky slid across the bench seat, opened the door for him, and then took his suitcase. She tossed it behind the seat.

He rolled the window down, then slid onto the seat and shut the door. He held the pistol out the window and snarled at me like he was playing a part in some gangster movie.

"Just stay right there, kid, and don't move until our tail-lights disappear. Got it?"

"I got it, Vinnie, but I wish you'd rethink this."

"Shut up."

He turned the key, and the car rumbled to life. Then he backed out onto the street and headed for town.

I took off in a sprint for our house.

As I jogged across the yard, I saw Mom in the living room window. She saw me and stepped toward the door. It opened just as I hit the stoop.

Mom's eyes met mine in a pleading gaze.

"Was she there?"

I stepped in, and she shut the door behind me. Granddaddy stood from his seat on the sofa. I took a deep breath.

"She's with Vinnie, in his car, and they're headed for parts unknown. I think you'd better call Detective Lewis now. Maybe he can locate them before they get too far."

Mom put her face in her hands.

"Oh, my baby, what is she thinking?"

"She thinks she's in love, and she thinks you've decided to send her to boarding school. I tried to tell her that hadn't been decided yet and we wanted her back, but she wouldn't listen. Just call Lewis, Mom, quick."

I put my arm around her and guided her toward the kitchen. Granddaddy went ahead of us. When we got there, he had the number dialed.

I heard Lewis answer, but Mom couldn't talk through her sobs. She handed the phone to me.

"Detective Lewis, this is Nate."

"Yeah, Nate. What's going on?"

"Becky has packed up and run away with Vinnie Marcello. They're in a new '55 Chevy convertible—red and white—and left about five minutes ago. Don't know where they're going, but…."

Granddaddy had helped Mom onto the chair at the end of the kitchen table, her usual seat, so I continued in a whisper.

"Vinnie is armed."

"Armed. Okay, with what?"

"Small pistol."

"Any idea of direction—north, south, east, west?"

"West, toward town."

"License number?"

"No, sir. Didn't get it."

"Okay, Nate. Tell your mom I'll get on this right now, and we'll find her. Okay?"

"Yes, sir. Got it."

I hung up. I walked over to Mom, hugged her, and told her Detective Lewis would find Becky and bring her home. She clung to me for a minute, then relaxed. Granddaddy took over, so I stepped out the backdoor to take care of Superman.

The next morning, I ran my route and got into a tugging match with the Lawsons' mutt that left another hole in the leg of my jeans. Then Charlie and I went to school, but without another incident with Tom Ray. Mom went to work so she could be there if they found Becky, and Granddaddy stayed in the house in case she called.

At school, I asked around, and Beth, the blonde on the swings the day before who couldn't make it to the party, said she knew Bones' sister, a fifth grader, and they lived in her neighborhood. I got the address.

As soon as school was out, Charlie and I mounted up and headed for the police department. Charlie had finally come up with the missing kernel of candy corn and promised he had it with him. That was important, but I wanted to see how Mom was doing, plus I also wanted to get the Bones information to Detective Lewis. I also wanted to know what the coroner had to say about our corpse.

At the SPPD, both patrol cars were missing from their parking spaces, and Mom was the only one in the office. She said the chief and Lum were out checking on roadblocks, and Lewis was looking for Vinnie's car. Mom had dark circles under her eyes, a tissue in her hand, and a box of tissues in front of her.

I had just told her about Bones when the door opened, and Lewis entered. He removed his fedora.

"Sorry, Connie, no news yet,"

He asked Charlie and me to follow him into his office. His eyes looked as tired as his wrinkled white shirt, green tie, and gray slacks.

We sat in the chairs in front of his desk, and he flopped onto his wooden swivel chair. He tossed his fedora onto the corner of his desk and looked up.

"I hope you've got something for me, boys, because so far we've got nothing."

I leaned forward with my elbows on the arms of the chair.

"I've got something for you, sir, but first, Charlie has something related to the murder."

Charlie leaned over and handed him the kernel of candy corn.

"I found this at the crime scene, plus we suspect Superman had eaten one or two more kernels when he was there that first afternoon."

He examined the kernel, slipped it into an envelope, then looked up.

"Candy corn, fountain pen, and a blood spot; that's good work, boys. Thanks."

I reached out and handed him a slip of paper.

"As for the Becky case, that's the address for Bones Meecham. He's Vinnie's best friend and probably one of the two teens that removed the body from Barrow's woods. He might know where Vinnie would go."

He snapped the paper with his finger.

"Great. I'll go get this guy right now."

Fifteen minutes later, Lewis entered with Bones in tow. Bones wore a black collared shirt with rolled-up long sleeves and worn jeans with tapered legs. His shoulders slumped when he saw us, then Lewis led him into his office and invited me to join them. Charlie stayed with Mom.

Bones, in a barely audible whisper, said Vinnie's family had a cabin on a fishing lake north of Pinehurst. He also had a cousin in High Point, but he didn't know the address. Other than the fact that Vinnie wasn't at home when he called him after school and hadn't been in touch with him, he didn't know anything else. But when asked point-blank if Vinnie was armed, he shrugged.

"If you call a zip gun being armed, then yes, he's armed."

Lewis leaned onto his desk.

"Where did he get a zip gun?"

"Jersey. He bought it from his cousin when he was up there last summer."

I looked at Lewis.

"What's a zip gun?"

"Homemade pistol that shoots one .22 caliber bullet. If it doesn't blow up in your face."

Bones pointed at Lewis.

"This one is good for more than that. Cost a bundle."

Lewis pointed back.

"How do you know that, Meecham?"

He lowered his head again.

"Ah, well, I just know."

I poked him on the shoulder.

"Did you and Vinnie sh—"

Lewis held out his palm and shook his head.

I nodded, but it also occurred to me that Vinnie's zip gun might be one of the other "cool things" Becky referred to last Friday night in the kitchen.

"Wait right here, boys."

Lewis stepped to the door and opened it.

"Connie? We have a lead on where they might be, so please call Pinehurst PD and get a list of all the lakes with cabins north of Pinehurst. And make sure they have the APB on Vinnie's car. They may want to go look for themselves. If so, have them call me for details. And get the chief on the radio and ask him to start for Pinehurst as soon as possible or ask him if he wants me to go."

He sat at his desk again and took the yellow pad from his desk drawer. He leaned toward Bones.

"What's your full name?"

"Jesse Tatum Meecham."

"Address and phone number?"

"610 South Ashe Street, 5-9929."

"Is your mom or dad at home?"

"Nah. Ma's working at the bakery, and Dad's on the road. He's a truck driver."

"Where were you last Friday after school?"

Lewis glanced at me, then back to Bones.

"And I already know, Meecham, so don't try to jerk me around. I just want your side of the story."

"With Vinnie."

"I *know* you were with Vinnie."

He leaned in closer.

"What were you doing with Vinnie?"

Bones hung his head and played with the bottom button on his shirt.

"Well, we were playing in Barrow's woods."

Lewis slammed his pencil on the yellow pad.

"I know you were in the woods, Meecham! And I know

you were involved in a murder! Now, are you going to tell me about it, or do I turn you over to the FBI?"

Bones glanced at me, then looked at Lewis and nodded toward me.

Lewis turned.

"Nate, would you leave us for a minute?"

I stood.

"Yes, sir."

I shot a look at Bones and left.

Mom had the phone to her ear, a pencil in her hand, and a yellow pad covered in notes in front of her. She gestured for me to sit at the duty officer's desk.

"That's right," she said, then she smiled. "Thank you, Mrs. Hall." She hung up.

"What's up, Mom?"

"The Pinehurst police have been very helpful. Mrs. Hall, their secretary, has given me a list of the lakes up there with cabins, but only one of them is north of town."

Her eyes brightened.

"And her chief has a cabin on that very lake. He's on his way up there now."

"How about Chief McDonald?"

"He's on his way here to drop off Officer Lum, and then he's going up there."

"No more roadblocks?"

"No, the State Patrol has taken over the search. We're off the case."

Fifteen minutes later, after Charlie and I had finished our Cokes, we got the call: No '55 Chevy of any color was at the lake. Mom knocked on Lewis's door, told him, then called the chief on the radio and told him.

A few minutes after that, Lewis came out with a yellow note. He handed it to Mom.

"Please call Mrs. Meecham at this number and tell her she can pick up her son here after work."

He tossed me a nickel.

"Get a Coke for Meecham, Nate. And bring Charlie in with you."

When we delivered the Coke, Lewis asked Charlie to stay and watch Bones, who sat slumped with his face in his hands.

Charlie crossed his arms over his denim jacket and leaned against the file cabinets. I put the Coke on the desk in front of Bones and left with Lewis.

Outside Lewis's office, Lewis, Mom, and I gathered by the door to the cells. Lewis leaned his arm against the wall.

"Meecham believes Vinnie killed the guy with a shot from his zip gun, and Vinnie believes he killed the guy, but I know for a fact he didn't."

I leaned in.

"You know? For sure?"

"For sure. That scenario doesn't match the coroner's report—a .22 bullet, yes, but a zip gun, no."

He sighed.

"Vinnie was showing off for Meecham and fired his zip gun at a tree. When they went to see if it hit the tree, they saw the body, and Vinnie assumed he'd done it. Apparently, Vinnie's not the sharpest tool in the shed. The problem is, according to Meecham, Vinnie believes he's a murderer and he's facing the chair."

I pointed at him.

"So that's why they were moving the body."

"Yeah, Becky called Vinnie after you called me Friday evening and told him you'd found a body in Barrow's woods and had called the police. That's when Vinnie told her he'd killed the guy. Before we got there with the chief, Vinnie and Meecham went back to move the body to the carriage house but weren't strong enough to get it into the loft. It fell behind the bushes, so in the darkness, they just left it."

"Were they the ones that shot at us Saturday?"

"Yeah, but not to hit you, just scare you. Once again, Becky told them you were coming. She ran to Vinnie's house, and the three of them went into the woods to see if you would find the body again. When you did, Vinnie fired at the carriage house, showing off again. They thought it was really funny the way you kids took off running."

"It sure wasn't funny to us."

I cocked my head.

"But how did it get in the lake?"

"They went back to the carriage house in the rain Saturday after a movie date to see *The Blackboard Jungle*, then they backed Vinnie's car up to the carriage house and loaded the corpse into the trunk. They let it rot until Sunday night when Vinnie and Meecham decided the smell was too much and they'd better get rid of it, so they drove to Aberdeen Lake. They dumped it at the head of the lake, but the runoff from upstream must have washed it down by the pier."

"Okay, but how did Vinnie know the body had been found in the lake? Becky didn't know."

"Meecham lied when he said Vinnie wasn't home when he called him after school. He was home, and they talked. Vinnie told him they were cruising in his car trying to decide what to do about Becky running away when they saw me go by with the flasher and siren going. They followed me to the lake and saw the coroner arrive and pick up the body. Then Vinnie decided he needed to run too."

Mom put her hand on Lewis's arm.

"Dan, then Becky also believes Vinnie killed the guy?"

Lewis nodded.

"Afraid so."

I held up my hand.

"Wait. If Vinnie didn't do it, then we're back to my guy,

generous with his Hershey bars or not. Could it be Mr. Barrow?"

It could be, if his pellet gun is a .22, or it could be someone else with a .22. And a motive."

I said, "How about Mrs. Urdenbach's husband?"

"What about him?"

"The other day, Granddaddy said the rumor at the mill was the husband might be back and he might not be happy about his wife dating."

Lewis took a notepad from his pocket.

"I didn't know about him, but I'll look into it. Meanwhile, I'm not pointing fingers at anyone, but the dead guy was Alex Hornsby, a textile union organizer from Chicago."

# CHAPTER 14
## SUSPECT NUMBER TWO

Detective Lewis went on to explain that he'd gotten a Missing Person Report early Monday evening on a Mr. Alex Hornsby, union organizer. Mr. Hornsby had failed to report to his office on Monday, and he had not been seen, nor had his room at the Jefferson Inn been occupied, since last Thursday. Lewis had started an investigation, and then he got the call about the body in the lake. The coroner identified the corpse as Hornsby and confirmed he'd been dead that long. Lewis also said Hornsby had candy corn in his shirt pockets like he'd been trick-or-treating.

A few minutes later, Charlie and I walked out of the SPPD and stopped at the bike rack on the sidewalk.

"Charlie, the dead guy is a Mr. Alex Hornsby, a union organizer. Remember the newspapers I saw in the carriage house that said Barrow was against unions?"

"Yeah, that's right!"

He stroked his chin.

"Kinda looks bad for Mr. Barrow, huh?"

"Yeah…kinda does."

I pulled my bike out of the rack.

"Look, we have permission from Mr. Barrow to go back into his woods, so that's what I'm going to do. We have a blood spot, candy corn, and a fountain pen, so maybe there's something else out there, something that would clear Mr. Barrow."

"Or convict him."

Charlie pulled his bike out of the rack, and I nodded.

"Yeah, I guess it could go that way too."

I looked toward the west.

"But we've got plenty of daylight left, so let's go. You with me?"

"Of course, I'm with you; paleface Kemosabe get lost in woods without me."

I grinned.

"Yeah, maybe."

I mounted up.

"Then after we do another search, I want to go to Bones' house and be there by the time his mom gets home from work. I think he knows more about Vinnie and Becky's location than he's saying."

He mounted up.

"I agree; I think that skinny little grease-ball was holding out on us."

A few minutes later, we rolled down Mr. Barrow's driveway

and pulled over at the rotten log where Superman had led me into the woods. Once inside the woods and at the edge of the clearing, I turned to Charlie.

"What do you think, one more pass around the clearing?"

"Yeah, I'll go left and you go right, but when we get to the other side, I want to take another look at that point where we suspect they entered."

He held up his pointer finger.

"But keep in mind, Nate, it's been several days, and with the rain and all, this might be a waste of time."

I nodded.

"I know."

Searching the clearing did turn out to be a waste of time, but when I got to the entry point on the other side, I heard Charlie, who was already into the woods, call to me.

"Nate! Over here!"

I weaved my way past a young dogwood with green-red leaves, then between a thin pine tree and a naked oak to where Charlie stood by a large pine.

He faced me with a big piece of bark in his right hand and pointed at a spot two feet up the side of the pine.

"Look here. See where a piece of bark was chipped away?"

I took a step closer.

He threw up his hand.

"Hold it. Don't come any closer. Look down over here."

He pointed to the ground between us and to my left.

"See the dent in the ground?"

He pointed to the ground between us and to my right.

See the scrape mark on the ground?"

It took me a few seconds, but I could finally see what he saw.

"Yeah, okay, I see both now."

I looked up.

"What does it mean?"

"It means the body was probably brought here in some kind of cart, maybe a wheelbarrow."

He leaned over and touched the chip mark on the tree with his left hand and held up the piece of bark with his right.

"Whatever it was scraped this tree, knocked this piece of bark off the trunk, then fell over on its side, leaving the scrape in the ground where the wheel skidded. This indentation in the ground is where the side of the cart or wheelbarrow hit."

He looked up.

"It was probably dark or near dark, so they couldn't see where they were going."

He pointed behind him.

"There's also a weak trail that leads off toward the back of the woods, maybe a game trail, but it looks like that's what they followed."

I squatted.

"So, if the cart or wheelbarrow fell over here and the body was in the cart…."

I reached down and tossed a few oak leaves aside.

"The body might have rolled out of the cart and onto the ground about here. Then…"

I pointed.

"Dropped this!"

I picked up a kernel of candy corn and held it out to him.

He took it, then looked at me.

"Okay, that may explain how it got here, but we still don't know who brought it here."

"No, we don't, but I know someone who owns a wheelbarrow. And they're close by."

"Mr. Barrow?"

"Yep."

"Ah, man, I was hoping he was in the clear."

I hung my head and studied the kernel of corn.

"Yeah…me too."

"Okay. He has a motive; he has a wheelbarrow; he has Wickers. But does he have a .22?"

I shrugged.

"I don't know…but he never did offer to show me that pellet gun, so I guess that could mean he was hiding something."

"It could, but I still don't want to believe he's involved."

I put the corn in the pocket of my windbreaker and looked up. The sun was just behind the top of the trees.

"I don't either, but we've got to go where the evidence leads us. What time do you have?"

He checked his Lone Ranger watch.

"About four forty-five."

"Let's get down to Bones' house and see what he's got to say about Becky. She's the number-one priority right now."

Bones' house was a '30s-style blue cottage on Ashe Street with a one-car garage in back. We didn't see a car in their driveway or any sign of life in the house, so we pedaled our bikes down his drive and dismounted. We rolled the bikes behind a large Ligustrum bush on the front corner of the garage opposite the house. We leaned them against the garage wall in case we needed a quick getaway and to avoid the sound of a kickstand, then we kneeled behind the bush…and waited.

At five-fifteen by Charlie's watch, a woman with a puffy pink face wearing a white uniform and white bib-apron drove a green Studebaker onto the gravel drive. She parked beside the front porch. Bones sat slumped on the passenger side. They got out and walked toward the porch, where we lost sight of them.

Charlie and I rushed to the side of the house and decided to listen first and only knock if we had to.

A few seconds later, a light appeared in the slightly-opened kitchen window above us, and a loud woman's voice called out.

"Okay, but then get back in here."

Then she hollered, "Faye, you home?"

From the back of the house, a girl's voice answered.

"Yeah, Ma. Doing homework."

A minute later, we heard a commode flush from the other side of the house. Then footsteps in the kitchen.

"Sit down, Jesse. Now, are you going to tell me about it?"

A quick scraping sound, like a chair across the floor.

"Nothin' to tell, Ma. They don't have anything on me. I didn't do anything."

A heavier chair-scooting sound.

"But that detective guy said you were with Vinnie, and he did something, tampering with evidence in a crime or something."

"Golly, Ma, it's no big deal. Vinnie thought he'd shot a guy with his zip gun, but he didn't. Somebody else did it. The cops know that."

Another scraping sound across the floor.

"So what evidence were you boys messin' with?"

A squeak, like a chair seat, then something clattered, like a coffee cup in a saucer.

"Vinnie thought he'd killed the guy, so he wanted to hide the body. We did."

"And they found the body?"

"Yeah, last night."

"Did they interrogate Vinnie?"

"No, he skipped."

"Skipped to where?"

"I don't know. I thought I knew and told them, but he

wasn't there. They know he didn't do it, but he doesn't know he didn't do it, so he's on the lam."

"That's stupid! Damn, Jesse, that Vinnie does some stupid stuff."

A metallic clatter, like a spoon in a sugar bowl.

"You need to find him and tell him it's okay."

"I would if I could, but honest, Ma, I don't have a clue."

I looked at Charlie. He looked back at me and nodded.

With the sun now setting behind the trees, we did the Sioux warrior/Osage warrior thing back to our bikes, then we mounted up and rolled home.

Outside our house, in the last light from a creamy-gray sunset, we decided there wasn't anything else we could do on the Becky case until the next day, so Charlie pedaled for home.

Meanwhile, Superman needed some exercise and chow. It was while I was watching him run around in the backyard that it occurred to me Mr. Barrow might know of some hiding places that Vinnie might also know about. I could use the "I've got an update for you" as an excuse to see him. He may have been against unions and own a wheelbarrow, but I didn't want to think he was involved with the murder.

I put Superman away, gathered my rocks and slingshot from the house, then mounted up.

On my way down his driveway, I saw Ollie glide by and the dark figure of Mr. Barrow, apparently bundled up with a hat and overcoat, observe him from his widow's walk.

On the porch, Wickers answered the bell and showed me in. When I explained why I was there, he went to a box set into the stone wall by the bronze knight and pressed a button. Barrow answered in an electrically scratchy voice, then when Wickers told him I was there, he asked him to bring me up.

Barrow greeted me wearing a Sergeant Preston of the Yukon fur hat and a wool overcoat. The fall-like air had lingered, but I was still comfortable in my windbreaker, jeans, and tennis shoes. But I wasn't eighty-plus years old.

He handed me his binoculars and pointed to the tallest pine tree in sight.

"Over there, in the top of that pine. That's Ollie's favorite perch."

Just as I had Ollie in focus, he dove out of sight.

"There he goes, Nate! Now watch. He'll reappear in a second but go inside the tree to have the first course of his evening meal—probably a field mouse. And you won't hear a thing. Most birds have stiff feathers that make a noise when they fly, but owls have soft feathers so they are silent fliers."

And that's what happened. Ollie reappeared in the sky with something in his beak, then flew silently inside the tree.

Barrow patted my shoulder and looked at me.

"Wasn't that fun? Bird watching is a great pastime. Remember that when you're older."

I handed him the binoculars.

"Yes, sir. That was something."

We rode a small elevator back to the first floor and the sitting area. This time I sat in the leather chair when offered. After Wickers relieved him of his fur hat and overcoat, Mr. Barrow sat in the leather rocker again.

He patted his knees.

"Well, Master Nathan, what brings you here tonight?"

He smiled.

"Are you collecting for the papers already?"

I smiled back and shook my head.

"No, sir. That will be Friday."

I twisted around in my chair so I could face him.

"My sister is missing; she's run away from home with your neighbor's teenager, Vinnie Marcello."

He leaned toward me.

"Oh, Nate. Sorry to hear that."

"Thank you, sir. Vinnie was one of the teens you saw in your woods. He thought he'd shot the guy we found, so he moved the body, then stole the body, then dumped the body in Aberdeen Lake. So, he and my sister, his girlfriend, have run off. But he didn't shoot the guy. The body was discovered last night, and the coroner's report revealed Vinnie couldn't have shot the guy."

"My goodness. Kids. What did I tell you about Hollywood's bad influence on our young people? Well, at least he's innocent."

"He is, but he doesn't know he's innocent. He wasn't smart

enough to realize the body was stiff when he found it; therefore, he couldn't have done it. So now he's on the run thinking he'll go to the chair if they find him."

He shook his head.

"Is there anything I can do?"

"I hope so. What do you know about the Marcello family, and in particular, where could Vinnie be hiding?"

"I know very little. I believe his father has lived here off and on, and when he was here, he was active in the community: Catholic church, civic clubs. I believe he was in the Lions Club at one time."

"Could the church be hiding them?"

"I guess they could. I'll call Father Garcia if you wish and ask."

Wickers silently appeared holding a tray with a glass of iced tea, a hot tea service, and a dish of sugar cookies. I wondered if good old Wickers was related to Ollie.

As he set the tray on the table between us, I thanked him and picked up the glass.

"Yes, sir, please call."

"Wickers, get Father Garcia on the phone and bring the phone to me, please."

Wickers nodded.

"Very good, sir."

Well, even after Mr. Barrow explained the situation to Father Garcia and the fact that Vinnie was innocent, the padre was no help. He suggested contacting all the hotels, motels, and hospitals in the area. Of course, Lewis was in the process of doing that or had already done it.

I set my now half-empty glass of iced tea on the tray.

"You mentioned the Lions Club. Would anyone there hide them?"

"Oh, I don't think so."

He stroked his mustache.

"But the Lions Club has an old summer camp and small fishing lake northeast of town. It's on this side of North May Street, two or three miles out of town and a half-mile east. McQuarrie Road, if I recall correctly. It was a popular place in the 1920s and '30s. I've been to many a barbeque and fish fry out there, but it's been rarely used since World War II. That's when everyone went into the service. They're a larger group now, so I think they use Aberdeen Lake for most of their outdoor activities."

He poured his tea.

"Now, another thought. The Marcellos spent a lot of time at the Pinehurst Country Club; Mr. Marcello for the golf, Mrs. Marcello for the bridge games. That's a possibility. There are a lot of outbuildings on that property where they could hide."

He patted the arm of the rocker.

"Yes, and if they were desperate enough to live like raccoons, they could get food scraps from the kitchen at the club."

I tried to imagine Princess Becky living like a raccoon and eating out of garbage cans. In love or not, I couldn't see it.

He pulled a cigar from the chest pocket of his robe.

"I'd say Pinehurst first, Lions Club Lake second. But don't rule out the church completely. They may not be there now, but when they get cold and hungry, that's where they may turn up."

I nodded and stood.

"Thank you, sir. Good leads."

He pointed his cigar at me.

"You're welcome. And I'll do this for you: I'll ask around, check with some of my contacts. They may have heard something or seen something or have other leads for you."

"Great. Thanks again."

I turned toward the door.

"Nate, just a minute."

Wickers drifted in again with cigar snips and a lighter. He lit Mr. Barrow's cigar.

Mr. Barrow leaned back in his rocker and blew the cigar smoke toward the ceiling.

"Who is the deceased?"

"A guy named Hornsby, a union organizer."

He raised his bushy eyebrows.

"Oh?"

He rolled the cigar in his fingers.

"And the murder weapon?"

"A .22."

"A .22. Hmm. Time of death?"

"They think it was last Thursday night."

"Ah. Then it wasn't what Wickers might have heard Friday."

"No, sir. He probably heard Vinnie shoot at a tree with his zip gun."

"And Saturday?"

"Vinnie again. He shot at the carriage house to scare us off after we found the body."

"And Nate? Was that your sister with Vinnie in the rain Saturday?"

Still standing, I nodded.

"Yes, sir. She'll be fourteen next week but thinks she's in love."

I held up my hand.

"But you and I are the only ones who know she was with them. I haven't told anyone else. Didn't seem necessary."

He waved.

"Oh, I understand, Nate. Our secret."

He rolled his cigar again.

"Then, if the police know it wasn't Vinnie, who is suspect number two?"

"They aren't saying. They may not even have a suspect number two yet."

"I see."

He took another puff.

"Nate, I have a long history of defending my mills against textile unions. There was a murder of a union representative here twenty years ago. I was suspect number one then, so I wouldn't be surprised if I were suspect number two now."

"I certainly hope not, Mr. Barrow."

He leaned on his cane and stood.

"Me too." He turned. "Wickers?"

Wickers appeared out of the shadows.

"Show Master Nate to the door, please."

# CHAPTER 15
## SEE ANY BLOOD?

When I got home, I had a quick and somber Swanson TV dinner with Mom and Granddaddy, and then I asked to be excused. In my room, I sat at my desk and picked up my history book. The assignment was Chapter 5, "The American Revolution." I'd read three pages before I realized I hadn't remembered a thing. Becky was out there somewhere for the second night.

I put the book down, opened my desk drawer, then took out the map of Southern Pines, the one I'd used to plot my paper route.

*McQuarrie Road.*

There it was, apparently a dirt road that trailed off and ended at a small lake.

I took the map to the kitchen where Mom stood at the sink in Dad's old gray sweatshirt, a pair of faded jeans, and her feminine leather boots she called "booties."

At the counter by the stove, Granddaddy hung over the

hissing humidifier, which he always did before brushing his teeth and going to bed.

I stepped up beside Mom.

"Mom, thanks to Mr. Barrow, I might know where Becky is. Will you take me there?"

She put the last rinsed glass in the drying rack, then dried her hands on a dish towel. She turned to me with life in her brown eyes for the first time that day.

"Affirmative, Marine, let's launch."

McQuarrie Road was more like four miles out of town and not that well marked. It took a faded sign reading Lions Club Lake, with an arrow pointed to the right, to make us slow down in time to read the peeling black-and-white road sign.

Once on the dirt road, the overgrown grass and weeds in the center scraped under our Ford, and the potholes in the tire lanes bounced us in our seats. If we were on a wild goose chase, I didn't see the need to continue, so I asked Mom to stop so I could check for tracks. She did.

I took a flashlight from the glove compartment, then hopped out and shut my door. I waded ahead through the tall grass on the side of the road. Where the headlights lit the tire lanes, I took a knee, clicked on the flashlight for more direct light, and looked for recent tire tracks in the packed sand.

I found them, two sets, one going in, one going out, or maybe two going in. But I couldn't tell if they were tracks from new tires or old.

I walked back to my door and opened it.

"Mom, at least one car has been this way recently, or at least as recently as the last rain. When was that? Saturday?"

"Saturday. The Saturday I went in to work."

"And I couldn't tell if the tracks were from new tires or old. If a new car had made the tracks, I would think the treads would've made a sharper track than what I found. So, it may not be them. Do you want to keep going?"

"You bet. Get in here, and let's go."

A hundred yards later, I could see the road ahead bent to the right, and then tall trees blocked our view of where it led. I asked Mom to turn off her lights and just creep along by following the moonlight reflected off the sand in the tire lanes. That's what she did.

I tightened my lips and shook my head.

*Two sets of tire tracks.*

After we made the turn, we passed a swampy area to our left that may at one time have been the edge of a lake. Then we rolled into a cleared area of gravel overgrown by weeds and grass. Moonlight revealed a row of rotting railroad ties along the left side of the clearing that led to a lodge-like building. The lodge and parking area faced what must have been the widest part of the lake. Wooden steps led up the side of the porch. A dim light shone through the windows overlooking the porch and the one window facing us.

I held up my hand, and Mom stopped. Ahead, two dark

cars faced the railroad ties; neither was a '55 Chevy. We were still thirty yards away, but the one closest to us was a blue Ford and looked familiar. Both looked empty.

"Mom," I whispered.

She stared straight ahead as if wishing a '55 Chevy would suddenly appear.

"Yeah?"

I pointed to the first car.

"Isn't that the car that dropped Candy off at the party just as we got there, the one that stopped perpendicular to the parking spaces?"

She narrowed her eyes.

"Gosh, Nate. I don't know. Could be."

"I think it is, and I think it's the same car I saw at Tom Ray's house yesterday afternoon."

I put my hand on my door handle.

"I want to see what's going on in there."

She grabbed my arm.

"No, Nate. Becky's not here, so let's go."

"Please, Mom, I'm just curious. I think that's Candy's dad's car. He's a union organizer like the guy that was killed; only he's the local organizer. Monty told me about him during recess yesterday. He saw him at a street rally in Robbins when visiting his uncle."

"But a union organizer won't help us find Becky."

She sighed.

"Besides, don't you remember? It was curiosity that killed your father."

I hung my head.

"Yes, Mom… I remember."

I looked up.

"But he left his flight to check out a target on his own; he left without telling his leader and without a wingman. I've got you."

She slumped over and rested her head on her hands at the top of the steering wheel.

"Ah, Nate, I don't know what to do. I'm just tired."

I turned to face her.

"Okay, how about this… You've got to reposition for launch anyhow, so while you're doing that—quietly, Mom, very quietly—I'll scoot up to the window and see if I can hear or see anything. You know, if these are union guys, I may learn something that would help our friend Detective Lewis solve a crime. But if it's just two guys having a beer and talking football, no problem. I'll just hustle back to the car."

She raised her head.

"What if it's a man and a woman having a clandestine affair? Then what, my precocious preteen?"

I raised my eyebrows.

"I learn something about clandestine affairs, whatever they are, *then* I hustle back to the car."

She shook her head.

"Ah, Nate. Go ahead. I'll reposition."

As soon as I cracked the door, the ceiling light came on. I yanked the door shut.

"Mom?"

"Okay, I got it."

She reached up to the light and moved the switch to off.

I opened the door again and slipped out of the car. I eased the door closed.

On my way to the side of the lodge, and while being serenaded by a few hundred boisterous frogs, I felt the hood of each car like I'd seen the good guys do in the movies.

The first one, the blue one, very warm.

The black one, cool.

A few seconds later, I stepped over a rock border and duck-walked under the side window. I leaned against the wall and heard a pop, then a metallic clatter on the floor.

"You want one?" a man said.

"Nah, I'm still nursing this one," another man said in an older, raspy voice.

I heard a few steps, then a scrape, like a chair across the floor.

"Well, I'm overdue, been a long day."

A chair creaked. A few seconds later, the younger voice spoke again.

"So now what?"

"We wait for orders. I don't think they'd planned on someone else killing Hornsby and beating me to it. How'd that happen anyhow?"

"Not sure, really."

There was a pause like the younger one was taking a drink, then he spoke again.

"Libby had this little Halloween party. She and Hornsby were on the sofa together when she accidentally spilled beer on him. Hornsby—drunk as usual—jumped up, screamed at her, then leaned over and slapped her around.

"I yelled, 'Back off!'

"Then the kid came in with a .22 pistol and yelled, 'Stop it!'

"Hornsby didn't stop, so the kid fired. He may have intended to kill him, but maybe not. But when the idiot Hornsby raised up, the shot caught him right in the temple."

"Damn. Well, it'll take those Chicago guys a while to replace Hornsby, so we're still on schedule."

I heard a bottle tap on wood like a tabletop, then the raspy voice spoke again.

"Man, getting drunk at a party and beating up the hostess you're supposed to be in love with…crazy. I mean, that's bad form even for those thugs."

"Yeah, crazy is right. Did you know him?"

"Only by reputation. Very smooth with the ladies. How'd you get rid of him?"

"After Tom Ray shot the guy, he screamed, 'Get up, get

up!' When he realized he'd killed him, he put the gun to his own head.

"I grabbed the gun, Libby grabbed Tom Ray, and then we sat him on the sofa. It took a few minutes to get him settled, but even then he was convinced he'd be in prison for life.

"I fanned those thoughts, then talked him into helping me dump the body on old man Barrow's property. Barrow's been opposing unions all his adult life, so he'd be suspect number one. With his pull they'd never convict him, of course, but they'd believe he did it forever and leave us alone.

"We folded Hornsby into a wheelbarrow and rolled him down the street then to the end of the school property, which is behind Barrow's property. We took a path into Barrow's woods and dumped it."

He paused as if taking another drink, then spoke again.

"I have no idea how it got in the lake."

"They found it in a lake?"

"Yeah, four days later, my daughter bumped into it in Aberdeen Lake, during a canoe race at a Halloween party of all things."

Raspy chuckled.

"Ah, man, that's too much—good ol' Alex was iced during one Halloween party and his stiff was found during another Halloween party. If we told New York we'd planned it that way, you suppose they'd believe us?"

"I doubt it."

Another sound like a bottle on wood, then a chair scraped against the floor, and the younger one spoke again.

"Okay then, we wait. I'll let you know when I hear something."

A couple of footsteps.

Raspy spoke up.

"Hey, thanks for the grub and the newspaper. Disappointed I won't be reading about my hit, but maybe it's just as well."

He snickered.

"That is, as long as I get paid for it, it's just as well. And take care of yourself, sport. I did some undercover work for the company a few years ago, and look what it did to me. I didn't get this way at the barbershop."

"I'll be careful. Good night."

I leaned away from the wall and heard the squeak of a screen door.

*Uh-oh. Mom.*

It hadn't occurred to me that one of them would be leaving so soon.

I turned to run and already had one foot over the rock border when a guy in a white shirt and sports coat jumped the steps and jogged past the black car. He froze beside the rear bumper of the blue car. With keys in hand, he stared across the clearing.

Mom had repositioned the car on the side of the parking

lot opposite the lake. It faced away from the lodge and sat under the limbs of a tall oak tree.

He looked right at it.

As he cocked his head like he was trying to figure out if he was looking at a car that had or had not been there before, I quick-stepped to the back corner of the lodge and crouched behind a boxwood.

Meanwhile, the frog's love songs, backed up by a chorus of crickets, covered the sound of Mom's car engine and my footsteps. I glanced behind me.

A cleared area along the back side of the lodge looked like it could have been a gravel delivery lane to the kitchen, which, judging by the stove pipe sticking out of the roof, was at the far end of the lodge.

I scooped up a baseball-size rock from the border and sprinted down that lane and around the corner to the end of the front porch. I stopped and peeked over the steps.

The guy wasn't behind the car!

I stood taller and could barely make out his form walking toward Mom.

I set the rock on the top step, cupped my hands around my mouth, then hollered into the woods and away from the porch.

"Hey, Rube! Ovah heah, ovah heah, got a big 'un!"

I grabbed the rock, threw it as far as I could, and waited… splash!

I took a deep breath and looked for the guy in the white shirt and sports coat.

He reappeared, heading back and on the run.

I ducked as the screen door flew open. A thick guy with gray hair wearing a yellow shirt and red tie stepped onto the porch. A cigarette hung from his mouth, and a rifle hung from his left hand.

He threw the cigarette onto the porch, then reached back inside and around the doorjamb. A click and the inside light went out.

I slipped back behind the side wall.

The younger guy banged up the steps.

"Who the hell was that?"

"Damned if I know. Maybe some redneck out fishing."

"There's a light blue car on the far side of the parking lot. Maybe that's them."

"You know anybody around here named Rube?"

"No, I don't, but that car in the lot sure looks familiar."

It seemed like a good time to beat feet, so I jogged down the side wall, around the corner, then sprinted along the back wall for the car, which I could see as soon as I passed the kitchen's backdoor, but boom!

I ran flat into Mom.

"Mom," I said, gasping for air, "what are you doing?"

She held her chest and sucked in a breath.

"Looking for you, Nate. I got worried."

I pulled her along.

"Well, stroll for the car. Act casual. There are two guys on the porch we don't want to mess with. And if we get caught, remember we're looking for Becky. Just play along."

I led her toward the car, but as soon as we got into the lot, the younger guy appeared on the porch steps and saw us. I turned toward the woods.

"Becky!"

I looked at Mom and gestured by turning my palm up and wiggling my fingers.

She nodded.

"Becky, where are you, honey?"

I cupped my hands.

"Becky! Come on! Let's go home!"

We were ten feet from the car when Younger caught up with us.

"Hold it, people. What are you doing here? This is private property."

I gave Mom a little nudge for the car.

"Go ahead, Mom. I'll explain things."

He stepped between us and the car and held up his hand.

"No you don't, Mom. I want an explanation first."

I looked at my watch.

"I can explain, sir, but we're overdue back home now."

He scoffed.

"Really."

"Yes, sir, really. Detective Lewis is probably already at the house for our Tuesday night game of Clue. He's a big fan of Clue, but I usually clean his clock."

Mom pushed me.

"Not always, smarty pants. He got you last week."

I looked at her and shrugged.

"Okay, not always, but most of the time."

I looked back at Younger.

"You see, sir, my teenage sister has run away from home with her boyfriend, and her best friend, Jenny, told us they might be out here. The boyfriend is a creep, so we wanted to stop her before she did anything stupid. Granddaddy didn't want us to go, so we made a deal."

He scoffed again.

"A deal, huh?"

Mom stepped up.

"Yes, Mister Whoever-You-Are, a deal."

She looked at me.

I pointed at him.

"If we weren't back by seven, he would get Detective Lewis to come after us."

"What time is it, Nate?"

I held my watch up to the moonlight.

"Seven-fifteen. Come on, Mom, we've got to go."

She only got two steps toward the driver's side of the car when Younger grabbed her wrist.

"Just hold it right there. I don't know who you are, but you're trespassing on private property, and that's against the law. You'd better come with me."

Even in the darkness, I could see Mom's eyes flare and her teeth bare.

"Now, you just hold it, bozo, and take your filthy hands off me! You want to take me into custody, then show me your badge!"

She jerked her hand free at the same time I remembered I was armed.

He reached for her again, but Mom kicked him on his knee.

As he screamed in pain, I reached for the rocks and sling-shot in my pockets.

He hopped around on one leg several times, then chased Mom to her door.

I locked and loaded one round and fired.

The rock zipped by his right ear, so it wasn't on target, but it got his attention long enough for Mom to get a grip on the door handle.

I reloaded and took a step closer.

He grabbed her arm and I fired again.

*Whack!* Dead center, right in the back of the skull.

He spun around and hobbled toward me with curse words spewing from his mouth and one hand holding the back of his head.

Mom ran up behind him.

She swung a leather bootie at his ankle and dropped him on his face.

She yelled, "Get in!"

I ran to the passenger side, but just as I got the door open, a big hand gripped me on my right shoulder.

"Freeze, kid!"

Raspy pulled me aside and pointed his rifle at Mom.

"You want this kid, lady, then get outta that car and come with me."

He looked at Younger, who was getting to his feet.

"You okay, Kevin?"

Kevin Crocker brushed the grit from his face and sports coat and nodded.

"Yeah."

He walked over to us, then turned the back of his head to Raspy.

"You see any blood?"

"No, but I'll take a look at it inside."

"No, I gotta go, or the family will start wondering how long it takes to get gas. I'll just go straight to the shower."

I looked at him.

"Tell Candy that Nate said hello."

He backhanded me across the mouth, and I would have fallen if Raspy hadn't held me up.

Crocker snatched the slingshot out of my hand and threw it into the woods.

Seeing me slapped was the last straw for Mom. She coiled her body, then blitzed Crocker like a Chicago linebacker after a Green Bay quarterback.

As she blindsided him with a shoulder to his ribs, he let out a grunt, fell into Raspy, who stumbled backward, and I grabbed the rifle.

Raspy hung onto it, and all four of us fell to the ground in a pile.

Crocker jumped up. He grabbed my windbreaker.

Mom jumped up and gave him another kick to the knee, which dropped him again.

I hung on to the rifle, and then bouncing lights lit the fight scene.

A siren pierced the air.

I looked up to see bright headlights roaring at us.

Crocker got to his feet and ran for his car like a pirate with a peg leg.

Raspy left his rifle in my hands and sprinted for his car.

The Nash swerved left, then right, then slid to a stop behind them and both cars.

Lewis leaped out of the cruiser with a shotgun and fired one shot in the air.

Raspy slammed a hand on the roof of his car, then raised both hands.

Crocker let go of his door handle, sighed, and raised his hands.

As Mom and I jogged up and joined Lewis, Crocker sucked in a breath and looked at me.

"Damn, kid... You weren't lying."

I looked at Mom and she looked at me with a smile and those dimples Dad loved. I think both of us couldn't believe that, by some miracle, our lie had turned out to be the truth.

Still catching my breath, I turned to Crocker.

"No, sir... My mother has taught me that honesty...is *always* the best policy."

# CHAPTER 16
## SUPERMAN SPEAKS

The next day I went to school with a fat lip, a cut on my cheek from Mr. Crocker's ring, and a written excuse from Mom for my missing homework. Mom went to work with a bruised wrist. Mr. Crocker went to jail with a hitch in his get-along and a knot on the back of his head, and Raspy went free. He never did anything illegal except camp out on Lions Club property without permission, so after being photographed, fingerprinted, and fined enough to cover utility expenses, he was released.

Granddaddy only gave us a coy smile when we asked about our miraculous rescue and referred us to Detective Lewis Charlie and I were invited for another Coke with Lewis after school. None of us had heard from Becky.

Candy never returned to our school. Her father was charged with assault, attempted kidnapping, and failure to report a crime, but by the end of the week, a slick New York lawyer got him off with a $200 fine and time served. The Crocker family moved to Philadelphia over the weekend. Charlie wasn't disappointed.

At school, I got lots of attention, especially from Chipper. She said she was disappointed we didn't get to dance together at the party, but her Girl Scout troop was planning something for the holidays, which would give us another chance. And they did. But that's another story.

Tom Ray was charged with murder, but it was changed to accidental homicide, and he was released. He actually thanked me for helping clear him, but it didn't hurt that Chief Mc-Donald turned out to be his uncle.

A week later, I saw him downtown at the hardware store. He held the glove I wanted after I'd saved enough money. I walked up to him.

"Hi, Tom Ray. Nice glove. I wish I had one like that."

"Yeah, me too."

He pointed at a blue Schwinn bicycle in the store window.

"But I'd rather have one of those."

That simple conversation led me to offer him a split on the paper route. He helped me roll and wrap, and then he would walk and deliver the papers on my block and his. Thanks to a generous weekly tip from Mr. Barrow, which I split with Tom Ray, I eventually had enough money saved to buy my glove, and he was able to buy his bike.

The bike was a used Sears J.C. Higgins model, but it did the job and we were able to split the route and the money fifty-fifty from there on. I never had to deal with Lawson's mutt again. Plus, with the extra help, I was able to add four new customers and get that baseball bat from Mr. Glenn. I was ready for spring. But that's also another story.

After school, Charlie and I pedaled down to the police station. Mom joined us in Lewis's office where Charlie and I sat with a Coke in our hands. Mom stood by the file cabinets and smiled when I leaned toward Lewis and asked for an answer to the mystery.

"How did you know?"

He pointed at me.

"Your friend, Mr. Barrow. He called me."

"Mr. Barrow? How did he know?"

"One of his contacts told him something was up with the anti-union guys. There might be a hit planned on the local union organizers, and they might try to incriminate him— Mr. Barrow.

"Another contact, a local farmer who owns the property next to the Lions Club Lake, told him he'd seen a car coming and going to the lodge after dark. The farmer said there was only the driver each time, so it wasn't teenagers going parking.

"Mr. Barrow remembered he'd mentioned that lake to you., so when you two didn't get home right away, your grandfather called me and said that's where you'd gone. I put two and two together and decided to check it out."

I scoffed.

"Well, for their sake, it's a good thing you did. Mom was kickin' butt and takin' names."

Mom shook her head.

"Not exactly, but together we were holding our own."

Lewis reached into his center drawer.

"Which reminds me… I've got something for you, Nate."

He pulled out a handmade slingshot exactly like the one I'd lost.

"I went back to the lake today to wrap things up at the scene and found this on the edge of the woods where your car had been parked. Look familiar?"

"Ahh."

I stood, reached out, and took it from him. I caressed it, then showed it to Mom. I pointed to the initials on the handle.

"Dad's."

I turned back to Lewis.

"Thank you."

He nodded.

"My pleasure."

Mom stepped toward the door.

"Well, come with me, boys. Dan has to get back to work, and I have to check in with the State Patrol."

As we left Lewis's office, the phone rang. Mom stopped at her desk and picked up the phone.

"Southern Pines Police, Mrs. Hawke… Becky! Yes, darlin'… Where?… Wait, let me write it down."

She dashed out a note on her notepad.

"Are you okay?... Okay, okay, I'm on my way. Don't move!"

Becky turned up in Albemarle, North Carolina, over an hour away. Concerned they could be tracked to a hotel or motel, she and Vinnie had bought camping equipment on their way to Morrow Mountain State Park near Albemarle.

They camped and played pioneer for three days and three nights. He couldn't figure out how to build a tent or a fire, so she had slept in the car's back seat, and they had lived off Wonder Bread, peanut butter, and Nehi sodas.

They spent the days yelling at each other.

By the third day, she'd had it with Vinnie Marcello, so she hitchhiked into town and called Mom. As Dad used to say, "Nothing like the great outdoors to bring a family together."

When Vinnie turned up at home the next day, and after a visit from Detective Lewis, his mother decided Vinnie would be better off with his father. She sold his car, and he was on the next train north. He never wrote Becky, and as far as I know, Becky never wrote him.

Becky was Miss Congeniality after that and became Mom's faithful friend and companion in the kitchen.

Granddaddy and I finished the iron lung in time to get his lungs in shape for their birthday dinner at The Holiday, and Becky said it was the best birthday she'd had since she got her Baby Beautiful doll from Dad.

While helping Granddaddy clean and polish the repaired

iron lung the night before Becky's birthday, I noticed the plaque affixed to its side. It read, *November 1, 1936. Donated to the Moore County Hospital by Southern Pines Mayor Benjamin Barrow, in memory of his daughter, Madeline, 1910 – 1916."*

I showed it to Granddaddy. He nodded.

"Yeah, I remember hearing about that. The daughter died of polio, and the wife died of grief two years later. He's been a recluse ever since. But as soon as the iron lung was on the market, Mr. Barrow bought one for the hospital."

After our little scuffle at the lake, which became known in our family as the Lions Lake Massacre, I saw to it that my friend, Mr. Barrow, no longer needed to be a recluse or watch for Ollie by himself every night.

Meanwhile, Detective Lewis saw to it that he would be over every Tuesday night for a game of Clue. When Mom invited him, he put a gentle hand on her shoulder and nodded at me.

"Of course, I'll be there; I wouldn't want Nate to look like a liar."

But that first night, the night we got Becky home and rock and roll was back on the radio, but this time at a more family-ly-friendly volume, I sat on Superman's sundeck under a crisp, dark sky filled with millions of brilliant stars.

With his head in my lap and my hand on his chest, I looked up and wondered which star would be Peter Pan's second star to the right. Then I heard the backdoor open.

I turned to see Mom step out. In a white turtleneck sweater, jeans, and freshly polished leather booties, she closed the door, then walked over and sat beside me.

She put her arm around me,

"Nate, I just want to make sure we're clear on one thing: We had to do what we had to do when we were dealing with those criminals last night, but in the future, when you're dealing with me, or I'm dealing with you, honesty is still—"

I joined in on the line I knew was coming, and we said in unison, "*Always* the best policy."

I gave her a pronounced nod. We laughed and hugged, and Superman half-opened his eyes and sighed a low-pitched moan of contentment. He spoke for all of us.

# ACKNOWLEDGMENTS

Heartfelt thanks go to my writing sisters: Julie Epps, a gifted copy editor and dear friend of sixty years, Charlotte Ainsworth, an invaluable reader/editor of early drafts of this book, Nancy Gross, my go-to junior-high-school adviser and semper fidelis sister, and Katherine MacPherson, a good friend, supporter, and writing cheerleader since 2004. Also, special thanks and appreciation go to Julie Murphy, a good listener and my inspiration for the character Chipper. It would have been a tougher slog without you, ladies. Hugs and thanks.

I would also like to thank George and Kenny Little of Little Insurance in Southern Pines, North Carolina. In 1955, when my family lived in Southern Pines, George and his family lived a block down the street from us. While I was writing this novel, George would generously take time from his busy day to help me remember what it was like living, shopping, and going to school in Southern Pines at that time. His memory is a treasure, and I am grateful to have been a beneficiary.

# ABOUT THE AUTHOR

Randolph Crew is the author of *A Killing Shadow* and *One-way Mission*, both military action-adventure novels based on his 793 combat missions. Now retired and mellowed (his words), he's having fun writing cozy murder mysteries for ages 10–110. His mysteries are set in Southern Pines, NC, where he lived as a junior high student with a reputation. For recreation, he enjoys hiking the great outdoors in his home state of Alabama. You can find him there or on the web at www. rcrewauthor.com. He'd like to hear from you.

Made in the USA
Middletown, DE
27 August 2022

72418860R00144